TI
LEAVING
PARTY

BOOKS BY LESLEY SANDERSON

The Orchid Girls
The Woman at 46 Heath Street

THE LEAVING PARTY

LESLEY SANDERSON

Bookouture

Published by Bookouture in 2020

An imprint of Storyfire Ltd.
Carmelite House
50 Victoria Embankment
London EC4Y 0DZ

www.bookouture.com

ISBN: 978-1-83888-138-2
eBook ISBN: 978-1-83888-137-5

To Dad, William Stanley Sanderson, this book is inspired by you and your piano. Never stop playing!

Each time I send her one, I send one to myself, lest we forget.

PROLOGUE

I'm too late. It happens right in front of my eyes. Tyres screech, followed by a bang, a gasp. 'Oh no, she's dead!' a woman says, and a deathly quiet descends. My heart thuds in my ears. Figures stand like lamp posts around us, and all eyes are on the road. Music pumps out from the house, lights blazing behind the shutters, but nobody is dancing any more. The front door is open, a gaping hole from which horror has spilled into the early hours of the morning.

The woman is right. She's dead. Her broken body lies in the road, her face frozen with shock, her lifeless eyes staring towards the car that hit her. A streak of blood is laced across the bonnet, the driver staring ahead, hands still gripping the steering wheel. Someone screams, and suddenly I unfreeze.

She gets to her first, and I'm close behind, so close the sticky pool of blood on the tarmac is right in front of my face, the smell of petrol making me gag. She feels for a pulse, but after an interminable wait she shakes her head.

The driver leaps out of the car and stares at the lifeless body of my best friend. Then suddenly she laughs, and claps her hands in slow motion, the sound echoing around the street. It's only then that I realise I'm still holding the knife, and the blade is smeared dark red.

CHAPTER 1

Ava

A buzzing noise wakes me, insistent, a mosquito in my ear. I slap at it, but it doesn't make it stop. The sheet is twisted around my body and I'm cold. There's no sticky summer heat making me sweat throughout the night. Mosquitoes like heat, don't they?

I open my eyes. No view of a beach from the window, no sun high in the sky. I sit up, let my head drop back when I realise the buzzing noise is my phone and it's the day of the party. My party. Exhilaration ripples through me as I visualise the evening ahead and what it means – the beginning of my new life.

I reach down for the phone, a list of things I need to do today running through my head. The text is from a number I don't recognise.

I've left something for you – check downstairs.

Is this a joke, a surprise?

I don't like surprises.

A familiar chill of dread creeps into my bones. It's always there, lurking in the background. *What if?*

I check the time. It's only 8 a.m., far too early now that I don't have to go to work. A surge of exhilaration rises inside me as I remember that I've given up the job I've been doing for the past five years. No more getting up at six before a fast walk to catch the 7.30 train to Paddington. No more flat whites at the station, sipping my coffee as I watch other commuters racing around. My schedule was crafted as carefully as the leaf pattern on top of my coffee; I always arrived at the café half an hour early, settling myself and planning the day ahead before the bustle began. Who knows what my American routine will be like? Bagels and coffee in a diner in Times Square, perhaps, watching the famous billboards flashing?

My dressing gown hangs in the wardrobe next to my party dress, a floor-length Victoria Beckham piece in electric blue with silver flecks. It's hard to describe how beautiful it is, even harder to believe that Ben personally picked it out for me and had it shipped over from New York. Excitement made me tingle as I undid the red ribbon with eager fingers, the tissue paper whispering as I pulled out the garment. The dress slid over my slight frame like liquid silver and the fit was faultless. He couldn't have chosen a more perfect dress. *Ben. Not long to go now …*

Sounds of traffic echo in the bare room. Now that the pale grey walls have been stripped of mirrors, the space looks bigger. Behind the white wardrobe doors the rails are full of empty hangers, the metal frames rattling against one another like hollow bones. Dad picked up my clothes along with the rest of my stuff last night and took it all back to theirs. Everything I need for one last night in this house is packed in my overnight case, which stands beneath the window. The surface of my dressing table is empty. My paperback is face down on the floor, next to a glass of water. It's one of Mum's favourite novels, *The Best of Everything*, and I'm racing through the story of four young women starting out in New York in the fifties, sharing their hopes and dreams. Soon it will be my turn. I can't wait. After tonight's party, I have one final evening tomorrow with my parents in an attempt to assuage my guilt at how much they are going to miss me, and then I'm off.

My mind returns to the text. *I've left something for you.* What does it mean? Is it Lena? But it's not from her number. As if organising this surprise party for me wasn't enough; I don't need a surprise gift too. Could it be from Ben? Excitement rises in me, along with the secret hope that he'll turn up at the party. But I'm scared to ask Lena in case those hopes are dashed. It's bound to be a going-away present, I tell myself; of course it's nothing sinister. I slip into my silk dressing gown and pull the belt tight as I try to convince myself not to worry.

Careful not to wake Lena, I push my bedroom door open gently. Hers is ajar, and I tread quietly on the wooden floorboards. She has spent weeks organising this party, and as soon as she wakes she'll be in a state of uncontrollable excitement. As will I once I sort out this niggle. I don't like niggles.

From the top of the stairs, I see something on the doormat. It's far too early for the postman, and anyway, it's the wrong shape for a letter. I step forward and then stop, gripping the banister. From here I can see it's a cardboard box, long and thin. I squeeze the banister with both hands, so hard it hurts, but it doesn't stop the way my pulse is racing. *It can't be.*

I pull the belt of my dressing gown even tighter in an effort to stop myself shaking. It doesn't work. I know what's in the box because I've been receiving them for the past thirteen years – ever since the day I can't forget, no matter how hard I try. One thing's for sure: moving to New York is definitely the right decision. It's the only way to escape.

I wish that right at this moment I was high up in the sky, seated safely in the aeroplane, England disappearing below me into a patchwork of green fields and toy houses, my eyes fixed firmly ahead, seat belt securely fastened. Far away from boxes slipped through my letter box, reminding me of my past. Whoever is doing this won't follow me all the way across the Atlantic, surely? Plus, Ben will be around to protect me. Though I'm hoping he'll never need to know what I've left behind. My stomach churns at the thought of telling him, and I take a deep breath. He doesn't need to know. Ever.

Heading down the stairs, it's like I'm walking towards the hangman's noose. I pick up the familiar package, knowing only too well what will be inside: the petals dyed an unnatural black, the thorns waiting to dig into my skin and make me bleed. I open it with fumbling fingers, hoping against hope that it's not what I think. A possibility as slight as the sliver of deep purple ribbon that holds the box together.

My hope fizzles as quickly as it was sparked. Black rose number thirteen. Dark petals conjuring up an image of death. I drop it on the floor and rush into the downstairs bathroom just in time.

The floor tiles are cold against my clammy skin and I give in to an uncontrollable shaking. This time it's worse, far worse. Because all the other roses arrived on the day of the anniversary. But that date has already passed. That date happened seven months and two days ago. In all these years, this is the only flower out of sequence.

And I don't know what that means.

CHAPTER 2
2005

Lena arrived with two oversized carrier bags and hovered nervously on the doorstep. She'd been friends with Ava for four years now, but had never been inside her house. Ava had been to hers more times than she could count. If Lena wasn't ashamed of the dilapidated council block she lived in, then what was Ava trying to hide from her?

She puzzled over this question as she stepped back onto the long drive and looked up at the vast expanse of house in front of her. Five bedrooms, Ava had told her, yet there was only Ava and her sister. What did they need all those rooms for? Jamie had to share a room with Dad when he was at home, but he'd been put away for two years this time. Lena would be almost an adult by the time he got out. She prodded the doorbell hard, in the way she'd like to prod some sense into her older brother.

'About time,' she said when Ava opened the door and moved aside to let her past. 'Butler off duty, is he?'

'Very funny,' Ava replied, but she grinned, and Lena smiled back.

'Are you sure your parents are out?'

'Of course. I told you. They've gone to spend a day in Durham with my sister. It's miles away, near Scotland. It's where she's going to university in September. My parents do love a day out. They'll get back really late and I told them I was staying at yours. I'm so excited.'

Lena had never seen such a large kitchen, with so many sparkling surfaces, apart from in the showroom where her Uncle Pat worked. And that was just a mock-up. She glanced through into the living room and spotted an upright piano in the corner, the mahogany wood gleaming.

'Don't tell me Martha plays the piano.'

Ava's cheeks burned. 'It's me who plays, actually.' She didn't think Lena would understand her intense desire to be a concert pianist. 'Have you got the stuff?'

Lena lifted the carrier bags onto the weird island thing in the middle of the room. 'My cousin got it all for me. I had to give him some money, though.'

'I'll pay for that,' Ava said, and took a ten-pound note out of a wallet beside the kettle. 'And my share of the drink.'

Lena couldn't believe that rich people left their money lying around – her dad kept his in a biscuit jar, but it was always empty. She unpacked the bottle of cheap wine and four cans of cider and put them in the enormous fridge. 'How many did you say were in your family again?'

Ava laughed.

'We can have a drink while we get ready,' Lena carried on. 'I'll do your make-up, I've brought my stuff. I can't wait to see Danny.'

Lena had fancied Danny ever since she saw him on the market stall helping his father. It was after school one day, when she was hanging out with Ava in the café opposite. She liked to watch his muscles flex as he unpacked the fruit, arranging colourful displays of oranges, kiwis, bananas and bright red apples. Creative, she liked that. Like her with her make-up. She wanted to be a professional make-up artist one day, painting the faces of beautiful Hollywood actresses.

'Who's that?' she'd asked Ava at the time.

'Danny Appleford,' Ava had replied. 'He's in my sister's Saturday drama class.'

Ava's older sister went to the private school up the hill. Ava had persuaded her parents to let her go to the local comprehensive, where all her friends were going. The headteacher had reassured her mother she would do just as well there. She was right – Lena could see that Ava was clever; she would succeed wherever she went.

'Hmm,' Lena had said, watching Danny. 'About the right age for us, then. Boys are immature, everyone knows that. So a seventeen-year-old is perfect. Apart from Gareth, that is.'

Ava pulled a face. She wasn't sure about Gareth. He'd hung around their group of friends for ages and everyone knew he was mad about her. She liked him well enough, but she didn't think she fancied him. How would she know for sure? Martha said that if you had to think about whether you fancied someone, then you most probably didn't. Not that Martha was an expert or anything. All she was interested in was studying and getting the grades so she could go off to university.

Ava was more interested in hanging around with Lena. Lena made her more adventurous; she was always doing impulsive things, like talking to boys she didn't know and giving teachers lip, and she was forever on at Ava to stop taking herself so seriously. With Lena, Ava could laugh at herself. Lena didn't have much of a family but she knew how to enjoy herself, and how to be loyal. She would do anything for Ava, and Ava felt the same. She didn't want boys to get in the way of all that. And being with Gareth gave her an uncomfortable feeling in her stomach. She didn't really want to go out with him any more, but just thinking about ending it made her squirm inside. How could she possibly tell him?

CHAPTER 3

Ava

Now that Dad has taken most of my stuff over to the family home, the house feels empty, my footsteps loud on the bare wooden floor, my pictures removed from the hallway. *WELCOME* is written in large letters on the doormat, but the image of the black rose is fixed in my head, making me feel anything but. Whoever has been sending the roses, it feels like they're getting closer.

The clip of my heels echoes as I cross the floor. The living room looks larger without my furnishings: the turquoise cushions, my Oriental rug and all the wall hangings. I didn't realise how much of it was mine. The bookshelves are empty of my books and knick-knacks. All that's left in the room is a brown leather sofa, an armchair, and some fold-up chairs stacked neatly against the bare walls. And my precious piano. Sitting at the stool, I run my hand over the dark waxed wood, trail my fingers across the ivory keys. Leaving my piano behind pains me, but my parents will look after it for me – after all, they've been looking after it for the past few years, when I was unable to face it. I've only been playing again for a couple of months, and just thinking about the memories that made me freeze whenever I sat on the stool, fingers poised to play, sends a shudder right through me. I blink hard to clear my mind.

I've spent most of the day on the phone, finalising closure of accounts and last minute business I need to sort out before moving abroad. The day has flown by, the sky gradually darkening, and

Lena's due back from work soon, and I can't wait; the moment she's home, we'll crack open a bottle of bubbly and get ourselves party-ready, painting our faces and twirling in front of the mirror like we've done so many times before. But for now, the house feels stark and quiet, and I crave some company. I switch the radio on.

Lena's been fiddling with the stations again, and Lady Gaga blares out. I'm not in the mood for music, so I switch to a talk station, hoping to catch something interesting to take my mind off the rose and the ominous text. Remembering that camomile tea is supposed to have a calming effect, I make myself a cup, inhaling the floral smell.

The early-evening news is on and I listen to the headlines. A stabbing in a London street, the blood of a defenceless kid smeared across the pavement, another tragic loss of life. This takes my thoughts into dangerous territory; it's easily done – so many triggers for unwanted memories. You'd think I'd be better at it by now, but today, reality has hit me in the gut. I've allowed myself to form the thought that has been wriggling in my subconscious: having a party is tempting fate. I'm convinced now that whoever sent the rose will be at the party tonight. And I can't tell anyone about it.

The text message is on my mind, a tangible link to the roses. Who? Why? Somebody from my past, it has to be. I hardly see anyone from my school days, apart from Gareth, but he wouldn't do that, it's not his style. The thought almost makes me laugh. Almost; I'm not quite there yet.

The weather bulletin follows; it's another unseasonably warm November day, more evidence of climate change. The possibility of rain showers. Not what you want on Bonfire Night, when you're hoping to use the garden for a party. I check my watch – only two hours to go until guests will start arriving, arms outstretched for one last hug before I jet out of here. How will I know if one of those embraces is a trap?

I push aside the thought, focusing on Ben instead. Lena wouldn't tell me whether he is coming, but a tingle of excitement runs through me at the thought that I might be seeing him tonight. That's more like it. All I have to do is forget the roses for a few more hours and then I'll be off. The Great Escape is how I think of it. The two of us hand in hand, wandering through the busy New York streets, me looking up in awe at the towering skyscrapers; yellow cabs honking and people hurrying past talking in strident American accents. But my excitement is dampened when I think about our last chat over Skype, which didn't end well. There was a strange sense of unease between us that has never been there before. He insisted that there was nothing wrong, but his stiff shoulders told me otherwise, his floppy dark hair covering his eyes so I couldn't look for my answers there. We can sort it out later, I tell myself.

On the radio, a music track plays before the start of the next show. I take my tea and sit in the one remaining armchair, closing my eyes for a moment. I blink them straight open when I hear the new presenter's voice. It's Martha.

As her clear tones jump out at me, I'm transported back to the last words she said to me. The words that have haunted me ever since. *She's trying to take my place and you're letting her. But you'll regret it; one day you'll see what she's really like.* If this had been any other day, I would have carried on listening, unable to help myself, but Lena chooses this moment to get back from work, and I rush to switch the radio off.

'Party time!' she calls, slamming the front door and throwing her bag onto the sofa. She drops the carrier bag she's holding on the floor with a clink and rubs her arm where it's red from the plastic digging into it, then moves into the middle of the room and looks around her.

'God, it's so empty in here without all your stuff.'

'Just how we want it for the party,' I say.

Last night, over a cocktail in the bar down the road, I was unable to contain myself, the balloon containing the secret finally bursting.

'I know about the party,' I said.

'What party?' She arched an eyebrow.

'Come on, Lena. My going-away party, tomorrow? The one you've been not so secretly organising.'

'Thank goodness for that,' she said, letting out a long breath before laughing with glee. 'You've no idea how hard it's been.' She narrowed her eyes at me, sipping through her straw. 'Exactly how long ago did you find out?'

I considered pretending for a moment, then laughed. 'Months,' I said. 'You're so rubbish at hiding things. Those "wrong number" calls you were always taking, being secretive about your texts. Normally you just leave your phone lying around. Oh and this was the best one. Constantly telling me how much you were looking forward to a quiet meal on our last night in the flat, just the two of us. That's so not you. It was pretty obvious really, but I didn't want to spoil it for you.'

'And there was me feeling smug at having managed to keep it quiet. Still, it's better that you know. I've been dying to talk to you about it.'

For the rest of the evening we had a giggly, girlie time discussing the party. 'Great,' Lena said. 'Now that we can do it all together, it will be so much more fun.'

But the relief I felt at letting on I knew about the party hasn't lasted. I should tell her about the rose arriving this morning, but I can't face it. That would mean having to tell her about all the other roses too. Talking about it would bring it all back, and tonight is about forgetting and having fun.

The sky is already darkening outside, and I switch on the free-standing lamp and the string of fairy lights Lena has rigged up. 'Oh, it looks lovely. When did you put those lights up? They weren't there yesterday.'

'Before I went to work. Cool, aren't they?'

'Yeah, they make it so real.'

A smile plays around her mouth and she picks up her bag of shopping. 'Prosecco was on special offer,' she says, 'I've got a couple more bottles so we don't run out.' She adds one bottle to the bar area she's set up and puts the other in the fridge. She's bought enough booze for about fifty people. Spirits, cartons of juice, wine and fizz. The glass twinkles at me, liquids shimmering turquoise, red and amber.

'How many people are coming?' I ask.

'It's a surprise party, remember. You'll have to wait and see. I've got to leave you guessing about some things. Let's get ready now so we have time for a drink before everyone arrives. It's only just gone five, so we've got a couple of hours. And most people won't come at the beginning. Apart from Fiona, that is.'

'Leave poor Fiona alone,' I say.

She pulls a face and we both laugh. Lena thinks my university friends are all stuck up. I'd been looking forward to seeing everyone until that text arrived. I shake the thought away and head upstairs.

Lena is singing along to ABBA in her en suite when I come to a stop on the threshold of her room. She assured me she'd been packing, but her room is exactly as it's always been – the usual scene of chaos. Clothes lie strewn on the bed and some of her make-up is set out on the small table over by the window, the rest of it visible in the workman's toolbox she uses as a case. The sliding wardrobe door is open and I can see that it's bursting with clothes. Magazines teeter in piles and there are two stacks of shoeboxes. Our moving-out deadline is barely twenty-four hours away.

She appears in her bathrobe, towelling her long dark hair. The light picks out the chestnut highlights.

'Lena, you haven't even started packing,' I say. 'We've got to be out by tomorrow evening, and you'll have a hangover after the party.'

'Stop fussing, I'll be fine. Don't spoil this, please. I've been looking forward to us getting ready together.'

For the last time lies unsaid between us, but looking into her amber eyes I can see that's what she's thinking.

Lena's room is spacious, but there's nowhere to sit. How can she bear to live like this? I make space for myself amongst all the strewn clothes, and watch her applying her make-up. She's attaching false eyelashes, her mouth open as she concentrates.

'Goldfish,' I say, regurgitating an old joke.

'Funny.'

The window is open and a cold breeze blows in.

'I was hoping it would be nice enough to use the garden.'

'It is November.'

'Yes, but the weather has been so mild lately. It was raining earlier today.'

'A bit of rain wouldn't put people off. Nothing is going to spoil this party.' She gets up, tightening her bathrobe, and indicates her seat. 'Your turn.'

I angle my face towards the window, and she switches a spotlight on and adjusts the angle. Whose make-up is she going to do when I'm gone? For too long I've been trying to encourage Lena to make proper friends outside the two of us, but she's always been reluctant. 'I don't need anyone else,' she tells me whenever I broach the subject. Now I watch her lining up her brushes, the tip of her tongue on her top lip, as it always is when she's concentrating. Does she really think that if she pretends me moving out isn't happening, it will just go away?

'Just like old times,' she says, and I hope the uncomfortable feeling those words arouse doesn't show on my face, which she is patting with powder. I shiver. She knows how I feel about old times. It's the real reason I'm leaving her behind and fleeing across the Atlantic. She sweeps her brush across my face with a flourish.

'Making new memories,' I reply. 'Am I done?'

She scrutinises my face, and I can smell peppermint on her breath. 'Done,' she says.

'OK, let's get our dresses on.' I don't want to dwell on the past.

I walk into my bedroom, where the silver strands of my dress shimmer in the darkening space. It takes moments to brush my blonde hair, sweeping it into a bun. Ben likes my hair down; that will be his treat for later. If he comes.

I hold the dress up against me and examine myself in the mirror that's fixed inside the wardrobe door. The woman reflected back at me looks assured and confident, despite how I'm feeling inside. I feel a rush of love at Ben for knowing the kind of neckline I always wear to cover my scar, and I run my hands over the expensive material, feeling as if he is right here with me. He says the scar doesn't bother him, but I cover it so I don't have to see the ugly raised skin in the mirror. That way, I can pretend it doesn't exist.

Lena is singing in her room, so I pull my door closed, open my case and take out the jewellery box, which is carefully wrapped up in a scarf. Once Mum had understood the surprise element of not wearing the engagement ring until we've made the announcement, she suggested I leave it with her, but I want it close to me. If I wasn't wearing my party dress, I'd have put it on a chain and tucked it under my clothes, enjoying the way my body heat warmed the cold metal as it hung next to my heart. A delicious swoop of joy makes me smile to myself as I open the box to reveal the large diamond set in a white-gold band. I slip it on my finger and hold my hand in different poses, loving the way the precious stone catches the light.

'Are you ready?' Lena calls from across the hall, and I slip the ring back into its box and rewrap the scarf around it.

'I can't wait to see what you're wearing,' I say, joining her on the landing. 'Oh.' I stop, shocked into silence.

'Ta-da,' she says, spinning in front of me. 'What do you think?'

The dress clings to her curves, accentuating her hourglass figure, and her strikingly made-up eyes are dusted in blue powder.

'I love it,' I say eventually, 'but it's the same colour as mine.'

'It's nothing like yours.' She pouts at the mirror. 'It goes with my eyes. I've used a more turquoise shade on yours. Anyway, nobody's going to be paying attention to me. All eyes will be on you. I'm sorry – you're not annoyed, are you?'

She's right, of course. It doesn't matter. And although it's the same colour, we couldn't look more different. Lena is only five two to my five nine, always wearing slinky dresses or tight tops with pencil skirts. She's cute and curvy and her beautifully made-up eyes stand out in her heart-shaped face, framed by her thick sculpted eyebrows. I'm tall and angular and prefer trouser suits for work and long flowing dresses. At school once we were walking across the playground arm in arm, as we used to do back then, and I overheard a group of girls saying what an unlikely pairing we made. Lena in her non-uniform denim jacket with her hair loose down her back, and me in my pristine school blazer, hair neat in plaits. Somehow, though, it worked.

'Have you got a plaster over your tattoo?' I say, noticing it peeking out from under her dress. 'Aren't you going to reveal it for the party?'

Lena got her first tattoo at the age of sixteen: a little star on her ankle. Since then, she's had several more, dotted across her body, each one a big deal. She spends ages sourcing the images, flicking through magazines in the salon or scrolling through Instagram, and never reveals the design until the tattoo has healed. They're normally tiny, and she's been keeping the latest one covered under her clothes, but tonight a plaster covers a large area on her shoulder. Her hair hangs loose, so it's barely visible.

'Not yet, no. It's not quite ready. That's why I've put the plaster on tonight, I don't want it to get knocked.'

'That's a shame; seems like the perfect chance to show it off. Your dress is great, though. I love it, honestly.' Lena has put so much effort into organising this party and I should be more appreciative. 'You look fab.' I fiddle with the strap on my dress, feeling a twinge as I do so. The scar. It does that when I'm nervous.

CHAPTER 4

Lena

When I woke up this morning, I wanted to pull my warm duvet over my head and not surface. Stay asleep, stay in denial. That way, today would never happen. But the thought of tonight made me abandon the pointless battle against time, throw off the duvet and step into the shower. What could possibly be better than a party?

Reality hit along with a burst of cold water. Ava was actually leaving. Squinting through half-asleep eyes, I fiddled with the dial until the temperature was bearable, mulling over last night in the wine bar, when she'd revealed she knew about the surprise party. It was a relief; preparing for it together would be so much easier, and heaps more fun.

To us, she'd said, her glass clinking against mine, and part of me still hoped she wouldn't go through with it.

The day at work dragged. I watched the clock as I trimmed and blow-dried and painted highlights into hair, and my clients told me about their children and their holidays. I nodded in all the right places, but my mind was on one thing only. The party. Three of my regular clients asked about my latest tattoo, which is hidden under my clothes but Ava will be the first to see it – and only when the time is right. As the afternoon grew darker, my excitement mounted, and I stuck in my ear pods, the disco beat pumping through my body along with the adrenalin in my veins as I dashed home, suddenly anxious to get the evening started.

And now, in just a couple of hours, the party will be happening. I run downstairs and stick on the party mix I've been compiling for months. When I open the cupboard to get out Ava's punch bowl, all that is inside is a solitary mug with an L on it. L for lonely. How I'll be once she's gone. Blood rushes to my head. I check all the cupboards, banging the doors shut, until I find a mixing bowl I can use instead.

I ladle fruit and pour juices and alcohol until the sliced oranges and cherries bob about in a rich red liquid. An image of a girl lying in a pool of blood flashes into my mind. *This is not that party*. I fetch a bottle of Prosecco from the fridge, needing a drink.

The loud music masks the sound of Ava coming downstairs. The colours of her blue dress shimmer as she moves, and the silk hangs perfectly on her pencil-thin figure, matched by her pointed blue stilettos. The material of the dress ripples like a waterfall. I was there when it arrived in a deliciously expensive-looking cardboard box, watching as she untied the red ribbon, unfolded the tissue paper, caught her first glimpse of the electric-blue fabric, so soft to the touch. She looks stunning.

'I can't believe Ben chose that for you. It fits like a dream.' The material is flecked with silver strands that shimmer in the light, and her honey-blonde hair is swept up into an elegant bun.

I glance around one final time. The lights cast shadows over the walls and the room looks poised for a party. This night has finally come. The piano gleams and I know Ava will have polished it again today. That makes me smile. Ava needs her piano, and I still can't believe she's agreed to be parted from it in just two days' time.

'When is the piano being collected?' I ask.

'Tomorrow morning. Dad's found a specialist firm. He'll come too, make sure they look after it.'

I grin. 'You and your piano.'

'I told Ben it's a deal-breaker,' she says with a smile. 'Either he allows me to have one in his flat, or I won't move in. Though it won't be the same as having this one, obviously.'

'I'm so glad you're playing again.'

'Me too.' Her eyes mist over.

'Taste this.' I ladle a small amount of the punch into two plastic glasses for us to try. She takes a sip and licks her lips.

'Delicious! Just tasting it takes me back to the first party we had here. Do you remember, when we moved in?'

'As if I could forget. You spilled a glass all over the carpet and we were terrified we'd never get the stain out.' Memories of other parties come tumbling into my head. 'It's more than that, though; we've made this punch at every party we've ever had together.'

'Don't remind me,' she says, holding the plastic cup so tight it crackles. 'This is the only party I want to think about tonight.'

I nod. 'Using plastic cups is so naff. The punch tastes just right, but it's such a shame we don't have your fancy punch bowl.'

'I'm afraid it's been sent off to Mum's, sorry.'

'The whole set – the glasses too?'

She nods. 'But there wouldn't be enough of them for everyone anyway, by the looks of it. There's plenty of stuff here we can use.' She opens the cupboard and takes out a random assortment of glasses, a few wine glasses and some larger ones. 'We can use these too.'

'You mean crap stuff. I wanted everything to be special.'

'And it will be, stop worrying. I had to make sure everything was packed up and sent to Mum and Dad's; the last thing I'll want to do tomorrow is move stuff. Especially if Ben is here.'

Her eyes sparkle whenever she mentions him, and I can't help a pinch of jealousy. I smile in response, biting my tongue.

'If he's coming tonight, he'll be in England by now.' She hugs herself and spins round, her dress shining along with her eyes.

'You mustn't call him,' I say. 'I don't want him to know you've found out about the surprise. I promised him you wouldn't. And he won't be in touch with you either; it's the rules.' I've told him not to contact her, to keep her in suspense. My cheeks flush as I think about his last message to me, and I shake my hair out.

'I haven't heard from him at all today,' Ava says, bringing me out of my daydream. 'Which is a bit odd. I don't know where my phone is, actually. Have you seen it?'

'No, not recently. Have you—'

The doorbell rings and we look at one another.

'It's too early for guests,' I say. 'I told people seven, earliest. I haven't even got my shoes on yet.'

'Probably my parents. I'll get it,' Ava says as she goes into the hall.

I turn the music off and move to the window, looking out at the street. A teenage girl hurries past carrying an umbrella. A man walks his dog. A mother pushes a pram. Life carries on as if nothing is about to change. I lean in so close my breath mists the glass, but I can't see who rang the doorbell. Then I hear the front door click and an exclamation, surprise in Ava's voice. I wait for more voices, a conversation, but there's nothing. The whole house is quiet, but it won't be for much longer. Excitement flickers inside me. Ava may have found out about the party, but I have other little surprises planned for her.

I go into the hall, full of anticipation. Ava is on the pavement outside, looking up and down the road.

'Who is it?' I ask, before yelling out as I stand on what feels like a needle. Grabbing my foot, I look at the floor. A battered rose lies on the doorstep, and I can see a thorn protruding from my foot.

Ava rushes back. 'What's the matter?' she asks.

'I trod on that manky old rose. What's it doing there? Jeez, that hurt.'

Ava stares down at it, her face as pale as the rose is dark.

'Ava?'

She pulls a tissue from her pocket, clears her throat. 'Sit down, let me have a look.'

Her cold fingers tickle my foot as she carefully pulls the thorn out. My blood is smeared on her fingers, a smudge of dark red, and I take the tissue, holding it against the wound, wishing I could use it to wipe away the image it conjures up of another party, blood pooling on the floor.

'It's only a scratch,' she says, but I swear I can hear a wobble in her voice. 'I'll get you a plaster.' I hear water running in the kitchen, and then she's back.

'What's with the rose?' I ask. 'I've never seen a black one before. It must be dyed.'

'I don't know,' she says. 'Whoever rang the bell must have left it on the doorstep, but I didn't see who it was.' Her face is still pale.

'Was there a note with it?'

'No.'

'It's a flower,' I say. 'That's a nice thing, right? Black is most definitely odd, though. Could it be from a goth?' But my joke doesn't raise even a ghost of a smile.

'I don't know any goths.'

I reach out and grab her hand. 'Are you OK?' I ask.

She nods, avoiding my eyes.

'Maybe you'll find out what it means later. Maybe there'll even be another surprise,' I say, trying to encourage a smile.

'I hate surprises,' she says. 'Apart from the party, of course.'

'Well there was no way I was letting you leave without a party,' I say. But I see through her attempt to placate me, the comment about the party hastily tacked on, and I'm puzzled at the vehemence in her voice.

I throw the rose into the bin at the front of the house. When I come back inside, Ava has wandered into the living room and is staring out of the window, her arms wrapped tightly around herself. I can see she has tears in her eyes.

'Come here,' I say, guiding her to the sofa. 'What's the matter? Why has that rose upset you so much?'

'It hasn't. It's just …' A tear slides down her cheek and she lets out a sob. I sit close beside her and hug her to me. Her familiar Lancôme fragrance tickles my nose, and suddenly I'm inhaling years of memories of Ava being close to me, forever by my side.

'Let it all out,' I say. I know what this is. It must finally be hitting her, this massive upheaval in her life. It's overwhelmed her like a tsunami. The mascara I put on her so carefully earlier has smudged, and I dab my finger at the black mark, rubbing it away. 'I hate seeing you upset. It's the move, isn't it?' She nods. 'I reckon it's a good thing you're getting it out of your system before the guests start arriving. Cheer up, Ava. It's your party; you'll hate yourself if you let nerves spoil it for you.'

I hand her a tissue and she blows her nose before smiling at me.

'Thanks,' she says. 'You're right. I feel better now. I've wanted to have a good old cry for ages.'

'I'm not surprised, with the horrible time you've been having at work lately. You know I wanted to go in and thump Pete for how he's treated you.'

That makes her smile. 'Of course I know, and I love you for being so protective, but I'm glad you didn't. That would have made everything worse.'

'At least you don't have to see him any more.'

She dabs her nose with the tissue. 'Let's have a proper drink.'

'Sure you're OK?' I ask.

She nods. 'Definitely.' Colour has returned to her cheeks and she's smiling again.

She follows me through the open-plan lounge into the kitchen, where glass bifold doors open onto the garden. We sit down with our drinks at the huge oak table, and I can't help wincing at the thought that this will be the last time we'll do this together. Chatting over drinks is our way of de-stressing after work, and I'm going to miss it. We both will.

This party is our final goodbye to the house that we've shared for the past three years, and I know that despite her earlier wobble, Ava is glad I've organised it. Getting emotional is understandable. It's hard for both of us. We've been inseparable for so long. Ever since … I stop that train of thought and look out at the lights strung up in the trees, more like Christmas than Bonfire Night.

'Thanks,' she says. 'You know, this evening means so much to me.'

'I knew you'd come round,' I say, touching my glass to hers. Last night, when she admitted she knew about the party, she told me she'd wanted to slip away quietly. But I was sure she didn't mean it.

'You've worked so hard to organise it all,' she says.

'How do you know that?'

'I know you,' she says, and we both grin.

'Come here.' I hold out my arms. 'Lena hug.'

She's soft and warm and her hair smells of fresh lemons, and I don't want to let her go.

'I really do appreciate what you've done,' she says, sitting back down and twisting the plastic wine glass around in her hands. 'Have you invited Martha?'

Where did that come from? 'Of course not,' I say. 'Why?'

'Mum suggested it might be a good idea. Apparently she wants to see me, make a fresh start.'

'Really? When did she tell you this?'

'About a month ago.'

'But you don't want to see her, do you?'

She shrugs. 'I was thinking about it.'

'Why didn't you tell me? I really don't want her here. You know what she's like, she'll spoil the evening.'

'I didn't tell you because I knew you'd react like this. But you know, it might be a good idea. Ben agrees. Especially now that I'm going away.'

'Oh, so it's just me that didn't know,' I say, unable to hide how hurt I feel.

'Ben's never met her, so it's different for him. Just hear me out. If Martha wants a fresh start, then maybe she wants to apologise. The least I can do is listen to her. It's not as if I can forget her completely. Every time I hear her voice ... She was on the radio just before you got home.'

I take a sip of my drink, too quickly, and almost choke. 'But you'll be in America. There's no danger of catching her plummy tones over there.'

'She's my sister, Lena. The only one I'll ever have.'

I turn away from her, her words stabbing at me. 'Soul sisters', we've always called ourselves, but she appears to have forgotten. Will she forget about me altogether when she moves to New York? My glass feels small in my hand and I imagine crushing it flat.

'These glasses are so tiny,' I say, finishing my drink and feeling frustrated that everything isn't perfect for tonight. I can't help my eyes brimming with tears. 'It's not too late to change your mind,' I add, trying to make light of it.

Ava looks away, at the bare room, stripped of almost everything.

'I still can't believe this is happening,' I say.

'Oh Lena, please don't make me feel guilty.'

'But we rely on each other, don't we?'

'Of course we do,' she says. 'And I'll never forget what you've done for me.'

'I'll worry about you over there, so far away.'

'Don't, Lena, honestly. It's a new chapter. I've got Ben, he'll look out for me.'

I nod, turning away, unable to look her in the eye.

CHAPTER 5

2005

Lena loved Ava's house. But Ava's mum was such a snob, and she didn't like Lena hanging around her beloved daughter. Just because Lena lived on the council estate. The visit to Durham was a godsend, otherwise Martha would have been at the party tonight. Some of her friends would be there, but they were mostly all right.

Ava put the bottle of fizzy wine and glasses on a tray, and Lena said she'd always known Ava was dead posh. Ava joked that she'd given the maid the day off. 'To get us in the mood,' Lena said as she opened the bottle with a loud pop, spraying Ava with bubbles. She poured, holding her little finger in the air like she'd seen on TV, and Ava choked on her drink, making the fizz go straight up her nose. Lena made her laugh so much.

Ava's bedroom was always tidy, but she'd made it look special today, stringing Christmas lights around the room. Lena said getting ready for a party was just as important as the party itself, which was why she'd brought the drink round. She was also really good at doing make-up, and she'd found a look she wanted to try out.

'Make me look beautiful,' Ava told her.

Lena thought Ava was already beautiful, but she liked her own looks too. They complemented one another. Ava was fair where Lena was dark. Ava's hair was long and poker-straight; Lena's was thick and wavy. Boys loved it, but she was only interested in one boy since the day she'd first set eyes on him. He'd noticed her, she'd made sure of that – got changed in the school toilets and put on her false eyelashes, then persuaded Ava to hang around the market with her. They'd bought cans of Coke and sat by the stall that served coffee and cake to old ladies in sensible coats and hats, shopping trolleys parked beside them the way the girls parked their bags at their sides at the disco. Lena wasn't shy, and when she saw him looking over, she went across to chat to him. Perfect timing, because tonight – only weeks after they'd first met – Danny was throwing a house party, and Lena and Ava were invited. Lena was determined to become his girlfriend by the end of the night.

'Can I open my eyes yet?' Ava asked. She had been pampered by Lena for at least thirty minutes. Lena had allowed her to take a couple of sips of her wine as long as she kept her eyes closed. Ava had done as she was told – she didn't want to spoil the surprise – but she couldn't wait to see what she looked like.

Lena kept her waiting another agonising few minutes before she announced that she was ready for Ava to look in the mirror. Ava almost didn't recognise the girl gazing back at her. She looked so much older. She'd never worn fake lashes before, and they were thick and spiky. The dark blue eyeshadow had a shimmer to it, and her cheeks were pink with blusher – or maybe that was the wine, she couldn't tell. She felt warm all over; whenever she drank alcohol it made her want to smile and hug everybody. She threw her arms around Lena now and told her she loved her. Lena laughed and embraced her back. 'I love you almost as much as I love Danny,' she said. 'Only he doesn't know it yet.'

After Lena had done her own make-up, a club anthem boomed out of the CD player, and both girls whooped, starting to dance.

'This is what they play in all the clubs in Ibiza,' Lena said. She was always talking about the nightclubs and DJs on the Spanish island; she planned to get a job at a hair salon as soon as she could to start saving up for a holiday. And Ava would have to come too, of course. Ava knew her mum wouldn't let her, but she wanted to go wherever Lena went; her friend was a ball of energy and she loved being swept up alongside her. Even if her mother hated it.

CHAPTER 6

Ava

The doorbell rings just as a dance track is playing in the background. Lena runs out to answer it.

'Sue, David, come in, come in. Ooh, what have you got there?'

It's my parents. I get to my feet as Mum comes in holding a cake tin and I feel a rush of emotion. Of course she's baked me a cake. Any occasion is an excuse for her, and she could rival Mary Berry with her fabulous creations.

'Are you deliberately wearing the same colour dresses?' Dad asks as he gives us each a kiss on the cheek. His old cord jacket smells of musky aftershave. I smile. 'You girls never change.'

'It's just an amazing coincidence,' Lena says. 'We're like twins, you see, on the same wavelength.'

Dad laughs. I'm really going to miss him and Mum. The thought of not being able to pop around the corner for a hug or a word of advice makes my stomach knot. And I'm trying not to think about my piano.

'Look, Ava,' Lena says. Mum puts the tin on the table and eases the cake out onto a plate that Lena has found in a cupboard. It's two-tiered and covered in thick chocolate frosting, with intricate white roses piped around the edges. It's beautiful, but the flowers make me think of the thorn in Lena's foot, the black roses that haunt me. I blink the image away.

'You have to go on *The Great British Bake Off*, Sue,' Lena says. They've been having this dialogue ever since the programme started. Mum's baking has always been in a different league to other mothers, who'd turn up with anaemic-looking sponges and misshapen fairy cakes for the school summer fete.

'Oh Lena,' she says. 'Will you stop. You know I'd hate to be on television.'

'Rubbish,' Lena says. 'I'm going to secretly fill in an application form for you.'

She would as well, I think with a smile.

Mum laughs and gives her a hug. I feel a twinge of emotion, thinking of everything I'm leaving behind, even though I'm so keen to escape.

'The room looks good,' Dad says. 'Shame about the music.' The current track has a lot of bass and not much else. Dad's always been a classical man; that's where I get my love of classical music from. He used to talk to me about the music he was playing and I've wanted to be a pianist since I was little. Maybe I could have been. My shoulder throbs and Mum moves my hand away from my scar, which I didn't realise I was rubbing. We exchange a smile.

'That's why you don't get to stay,' Lena says. 'You'd hate the noise.'

'Well don't go upsetting the neighbours.' Dad looks at the table. 'I might have known the dreaded punch would make an appearance,' he says. 'I hope it isn't as strong as that time Auntie Sally came round.'

We all groan, and Lena rolls her eyes. Dad never lets us forget the time my aunt overindulged one Christmas before throwing up in a flower pot. She's been mortified ever since.

'Dad, we're not teenagers. This is a sophisticated party. Would you like a glass of the punch, or something more adult and sensible?'

'Yes, what would you like?' Lena asks. 'I'm in charge of the drinks.' She indicates the bottles lined up on the table, which is covered in a silver paper tablecloth with golden hearts scattered all over it. 'We have wine, gin, vodka, rum, juice, Coke.'

'Coke, please,' says Dad. 'I'm driving.'

'I'll have a gin and tonic,' Mum says.

While Lena pours the drinks, I make space for the cake, the golden hearts shifting and shimmering around the tablecloth.

'What time is everyone coming?' Mum asks.

'The party officially starts at seven, but most people will no doubt be fashionably late,' Lena says, just as a van pulls up outside the house. I peer out and see a woman emerging from it with a box. 'And I've got something special planned around midnight.'

'What's that?' I ask.

'Ava … I keep telling her this is a surprise party,' she says to my parents, 'but she doesn't seem to understand what that means. Lots of exciting things are going to happen.' She leans in to my mother and whispers in her ear.

'Oh, that's lovely,' Mum says.

Dad winks at me. 'I suppose young Gareth is coming?'

'Dad …'

'Can you imagine if I hadn't invited him?' Lena says.

'Poor young man will be distraught that you're leaving, Ava. He's carried a torch for you for years.'

I roll my eyes, and they all laugh. In truth, I'm relieved to be finally leaving Gareth behind.

The doorbell rings and I freeze, the rose left on the doorstep still fresh in my mind. I sip my drink, willing myself into party mode.

'Looks like a delivery,' Dad says. 'I wonder what it could be. A cake to rival your mother's, perhaps? I'll get it.'

Lena grins. 'It's another part of the surprise.' She follows my father, and when they come back in, they're both carrying trays of canapés covered in cling film.

'Oh Lena. You've gone to such effort.' Tears spring into my eyes and I feel guilty about not being more enthusiastic, but the rose has unsettled me. Lena knows me so well; I'm convinced she can read my mind.

'Hasn't she?' Mum says. 'She's been planning this for ages. I'm amazed she managed to keep it a secret for so long. If she weren't so committed to being a make-up artist, I'd recommend a career as an event planner. Are you all right, darling?' She's noticed me wiping my eyes. I nod, swallowing back the tears.

The sound of chatter filters down the path and the doorbell rings before she can interrogate me any further.

'Looks like your first guests are here,' Dad says.

Lena goes to answer and comes back in with the young couple from across the road. We exchange greetings and Lena starts preparing their drinks.

'Thanks for the cake, Mum,' I say. 'It's gorgeous as ever.'

She pulls me into a hug and I sink into her warmth as she rubs my back.

'You look beautiful in that dress,' she says. 'Are you sure you're all right, darling? You seem a bit distracted.'

I gesture towards the table. 'It's all this. It's really sweet of Lena, but I'd rather slip away without a fuss, what with everything that's been going on at work lately.' I had to tell Mum about Pete when she was giving me a hard time about packing in a good job to move to an uncertain future. 'And she won't tell me whether Ben's coming or not. It would be so awesome if he was. Do you know?'

Mum glances at Dad to see whether he's listening.

'I can't say, love, I promised. You know how excited Lena gets.' She lowers her voice. 'But I don't think you'll be disappointed.'

'Ooh, thanks, Mum.' I squeeze her to me again, inhaling her lavender fragrance. 'I promise I won't say anything.'

The doorbell rings again, and Dad waves at Mum.

'We won't be staying long,' she says. 'You've got everything you need here, haven't you? And Dad can always pop over in the morning if there's anything you've left behind.'

'He's already arranged to come back anyway. There's a shelf of books and paperwork we couldn't fit in the car earlier. And he wants to supervise the piano removal. Did I tell you Ben's going to get me one? I've finally convinced him it won't ruin the look of his flat.'

Mum laughs. 'I knew he'd come round eventually. We're so happy you're playing again, darling.'

'Me too. I never thought I'd want to again. Mum, before you go, I just wanted to say I'm sorry I'm going so far away, but you do understand, don't you?'

'Oh darling, of course we do.' Her voice is thick with emotion. 'Your dad and I think it's marvellous. And we love Ben. Please don't feel guilty; you've had enough of that to last a lifetime already. Anyway, it could be worse; it could be Australia!'

The doorbell rings again, giving me an excuse to compose myself. My mother and I have always been close, but she understands why I need to go. It's hard for me to leave Lena too – we virtually grew up together – but the time has finally come. This party is our celebration.

A dog is yelping in the distance when I open the door, and a burning smell fills the air. Bonfire Night is one of my favourite times. Fiona, my old friend from university, pulls me into a hug. A car draws away from the kerb.

'I'm so happy to see you,' she says. Her shoulders are bare in her little black dress.

'You must be freezing.'

'I came in a cab so I wouldn't have to bother with a coat.' Of course, she's still wearing woolly tights and sensible Mary Janes. The same shoes she wears for her job as an accountant. I smile. She never changes.

Lena appears in the doorway. 'Fiona, hey. Let me get you a drink.' I feel a rush of emotion at the effort she's making.

During my first year at university, Fiona was in the next room to me in college. Over the years, she's become a close friend, but she and Lena have never got on. Fiona can't understand my bond with Lena, and often mentions how unusual our friendship is, given how different we are. I can't explain it to her. I don't talk about that time; it's how I cope. Lena thinks Fiona is stuck up, with her love of horse riding and her clipped upper-class accent, but I've managed to keep my friendships with them separate and so appease them both.

Lena leads Fiona inside, but the noise of fireworks popping behind me makes me turn and watch the yellow and green showers in the sky. A cold breeze blows, and I catch sight of the black rose sticking out of the dustbin. I march over and push it down as hard as I can, but as soon as I replace the metal lid, it springs out again. I shudder, wishing it would go away, along with the mystery of the sender that is never far from my mind.

I turn back to the house. Light spills out through the open slats of the blinds and muffled music plays. I watch the figures moving behind the windows and think of all those yet to arrive, wondering if the sender of the roses is amongst them.

CHAPTER 7

Lena

I open the door to Lorraine, who lives down the road. Immediately she swoops on Ava, who is chatting to Fiona, and engulfs her in an embrace.

'I can't believe we'll never run together again,' she says. 'You know I'll never get out of bed now that I know you're not going to be there, always at exactly the right time, without fail.'

'That sounds like our Ava,' David says. 'Ever the perfectionist.'

'Well you'll have to come and visit me and we can run round Central Park.'

'Oh, you darling. Don't you look fabulous? Shall we take a photo?' Lorraine pulls out her phone and grins at the camera, showing lots of teeth, her cheeks flushed. Ava holds her empty glass in the air. 'Do you want to take one?' Lorraine asks her.

'Sorry, I don't know where my phone is. Send it to me.'

'Let me get you both a drink,' I say, taking Ava's glass. 'What would you like, Lorraine?'

'Gin and tonic, please, easy on the tonic. I plan to enjoy myself tonight. We'll give Ava the best send-off this street has ever seen.' She raises an eyebrow at me. 'This is going to be such a great party.'

Once I've sorted Lorraine out and made sure the rest of the guests have got drinks, I check everything's how I want it to be. Tonight has to be perfect. It's dark outside now and I dim the lights so that the fairy lights sparkle like it's Christmas. Not that

Christmas was ever a big deal in our house; Dad had a drink every day of the year, so Christmas was more of the same. In the kitchen, the food is set out to one side, and I put Sue's chocolate cake in the fridge for later. A little thrill ripples through me whenever I think about what I've got planned. I'm so pleased the canapés were delivered on time – one less thing to worry about – but the plates aren't how I imagined. In my mind, I had it all laid out on Ava's fancy dinner set with the elegant silver edges. I let out a breath, reminding myself not to get agitated.

The lighting is right now and I start my party playlist from the beginning. No slow songs; pure dance music. Every song Ava and I have ever danced to – the soundtrack to our lives. Yelling out the words to 'Crazy in Love' in Lena's bedroom every day after school for weeks; listening to Christina Aguilera's 'Beautiful' on shared headphones, mouthing the words to each other; me playing 'Marry the Night' over and over at my twenty-first birthday party, Ava struggling to share my excitement. It was too soon, back then. The thumping beat makes me vibrate inside, and I see David wince, so I turn it down a bit. Ava's having another intense conversation with her mum, and I wander into the kitchen, where the bottles glint in my bar area. I'm going to miss this amazing house and all the memories we've made.

Looking around, I'm transported back to the day I first brought Ava here. I couldn't believe my luck when Kerry at work mentioned that her brother was looking for someone to rent his house. He didn't want to go through an agency; wanted someone he could trust. Kerry forgot to tell me about the designer spec, left that as a surprise. And what a shock it was. I knew Ava would fall in love with the place. I went to meet her from work that day, telling her that the property was made for us and she just had to see it. The location was perfect, not far from a mainline train station and the Tube, with access to both of our workplaces. The wide street was lined with trees and there was a park at the end of the road, perfect for running and summer picnics.

From the front, it looked like an ordinary Victorian terrace in a street full of similar-looking houses. It had a glossy black front door and a brass knocker. We walked through the long hall, with its high ceiling and stark white walls, moving left into the airy living room. White lights hung from the ceiling and the furniture was minimal: a black leather sofa and an expensive-looking chair. The room formed an L shape, leading into the kitchen, which gave the house its wow factor. A large open-plan space with pale grey walls and spotlights in the ceiling, globe lights hanging over the island in the middle of the room. Beyond that was a glass extension at the back of the house, looking out onto the garden, with a table and chairs set out on grey marble-effect tiles. Upstairs was equally airy and light.

We stopped off for a coffee afterwards in a hipster café in a little row of shops that wouldn't have looked out of place in Shoreditch. The street was home to artisan bakers and stylish boutiques, giving the place a village feel. Ava adored the area straight away, just like I knew she would.

'Are you sure we can afford it? It's such an amazing house,' she said.

'No need to worry about that. Kerry's giving us a special rate. I told you it was perfect, didn't I?'

And now she's leaving this perfect house, and all the memories we've made here.

The fairy lights catch the glass, and the pink and green liquids make pretty dancing patterns on the table. The room looks good, and I grudgingly admit to myself that the minimalist decor is perfect for a party, although the sofa looked better with Ava's cushions scattered on it, pops of colour against the dark leather.

The beat of the music makes me long to dance. I want throbbing music and moving bodies like the parties we used to go to, and I want to forget for one night why we are throwing this one. I don't want an evening of standing around and having boring conversations. The fireworks will help with that – one surprise I've actually managed to keep from Ava.

Back in the lounge, Sue is still talking to Ava, so I go over to David. I've always found him easy to talk to.

'Looks meaningful,' I say, glancing across at his wife and daughter.

'Sue is taking her leaving hard,' he says, 'but it's just the idea of it. She'll be fine. She's pleased Ava's found such a great guy to spend her life with. It's probably a good idea for her to have a fresh start.' He gives me the look and doesn't need to explain what he means. Since the accident, it's always a subtext to any conversation. 'And what about you? I'm surprised you're not staying in this fabulous house.'

'You and everyone else.'

'Where are you moving to?'

I shrug, watching Ava out of the corner of my eye. 'Stacey's flat. She's a friend.'

'You know,' he slings his arm round my shoulder, 'Sue and I have been talking, and we do understand how tough Ava's leaving is for you, but you have to let her go. She needs this break, a new chapter. It will be good for you too, trust me.'

His words catch me unawares and I reach for my plastic cup. So that's why they're not asking me to come and live with them. To toughen me up. I was sure Sue would have invited me by now, just like she did when I was sixteen.

'Ava mentioned Martha earlier,' I say.

'Oh yes?'

'Apparently she wants to get in touch.'

'And you find that difficult.' His eyes are kind.

I nod. 'I get it – I mean, they're sisters – but …'

'What's upsetting you?'

'It's the fact that she didn't tell me before. We used to tell each other everything, and I thought she still did. We're like sisters.'

'I know you are. Our family is indebted to you; that's why we took you in when we did. You deserved a stable home life after everything that happened. Martha isn't easy to get on with, but she has Ava's best interests at heart too. You both want the same thing; you just clash. You're very alike, you know.'

I pull a face, and he laughs.

'Careful, that's my daughter you're dissing.'

'She's not coming tonight, though, is she?'

'Not as far as I know. Stop worrying, and enjoy the party. You've done a great job.'

We both look around us. The fairy lights are flickering, casting pretty patterns across the walls and floor.

'Sue and I should be getting off now. We don't want to outstay our welcome.'

I grin. 'We'll turn the music up again the minute you're gone.'

'That's my girl,' he says, giving my arm a squeeze. 'Sue,' he calls, and she comes over. 'Time we were leaving. We need to let these young people go wild.'

'This isn't a rave,' I say with a laugh. 'Where's Ava gone?'

'She popped upstairs to look for her phone … Ah, here she is. Did you find it, love?'

'No,' Ava says. 'I had a quick look in both our rooms, but it seems to have disappeared.' She shrugs. 'I'm sure it will turn up.'

'Bye, everyone,' David says, and the four of us go into the hall. It occurs to me that I don't know when we will be together like this again, and I want to stop time, keep us all here where I feel safest.

David takes out his car keys as Sue gives us both a hug. Her lavender perfume is as familiar to me as Ava's, and it takes me back to that dark street where she put her arms around me for the first time, holding me until I stopped shaking and managed to tear my eyes from the terrible scene in front of me. But for how much longer will the lavender scent linger? Do they really want me to keep in touch? David meant well with his kind words, but he's reminded me that Martha is his daughter and I'm not. No matter what they say, everything is changing.

We stay on the doorstep until the car has disappeared from sight, but my feelings of unease don't shift.

'It's freezing,' Ava says. 'Let's go in.'

Back inside, I turn up the music, but I've only just picked up my drink when the doorbell goes again. This time it rings for a long time, as if someone is holding their finger against it.

'Maybe we should just leave the door open,' I say to nobody in particular.

As I open the front door, a high-pitched noise fills the air and a rocket explodes in the sky.

'Jesus,' says the man in front of me. He's wearing a high-vis vest and holding a parcel.

'Ava Thomas?' he asks.

'No, but I can take it for her. Do you need a signature?'

He places the box on the ground and hands me a device, which I sign with an electronic pen, my signature a flourish.

'Good party?' he asks.

'Yeah, thanks. It's rough for you having to work on a Saturday night.'

'This is my last delivery of the night, then I'll be partying too, don't you worry about me.'

I laugh and take the box, which is surprisingly light. I wonder if it's from Ben, but there's a UK delivery label on it, with no indication of what it is.

'Ooh, presents,' says a man, coming out into the hall. 'Ava, delivery!' he calls. He leads the way back into the living room, where people are laughing and chatting. Ava looks over from her conversation with Lorraine and comes across, grinning. Lorraine follows her.

'What's this?' she asks. 'Lena, you have to stop giving me things.'

'Not guilty. I just took this in at the door.'

'Maybe it's from Ben,' she says, and her eyes sparkle. We go through to the kitchen and I put the box on the table. 'He already sent my dress, though. I wouldn't expect anything else.'

'I don't think it's from him,' I say. 'It looks local.'

She gets some scissors and cuts the top.

'Who's it from?' I ask. 'Does it say?'

'I don't know.' She rummages around. 'There's no card, which is weird.' She lifts the lid of the inner box to reveal a single-tiered cake covered in black icing, a white band around the edge. Her silver-painted nails are a stark contrast to the unusual dark frosting. On top of the cake, piped in white icing, is the number 13. She gasps and almost drops the box to the floor.

'Whoopsy,' says Lorraine, holding out a hand to steady it. 'Do you know who it's from?'

Ava shakes her head in a robotic fashion, staring at the cake with glassy eyes.

'It's gorgeous, so classy.' Lorraine peers at it, oblivious to Ava's reaction. 'Although the black is quite unusual. Look at the detail on those roses. I wonder what flavour it is. And what does the number signify? Obviously it's not the thirteenth anniversary of you and Ben being together.'

Her words fade into white noise and I can't take my eyes off Ava, who is gripping the edge of the table, her fingers taut. One possible significance of the number has leapt into my head, and I gulp.

'I do love a mystery,' Lorraine says. 'You look as if you're in shock, Ava. Too much excitement, I reckon, I'll get you another drink.'

'It's OK, I've remembered who it's from,' I say, my thoughts racing, the lie tripping out. 'It's supposed to be a three, not thirteen, for the three happy years we've lived in this house.'

'How sweet,' Lorraine says, putting a glass in Ava's hand. 'Oh look, there's Yasmin. Excuse me, ladies.' She moves away and I take Ava's arm. She's shaking.

'Let's put this in the fridge.'

'Please tell me that's true, about the three years,' she says as a blast of cold air from the fridge hits us.

'I wish I could. I just said it to stop Lorraine's questions. You know how she goes on. I have no idea who this is from.'

'Oh God,' she says, taking a large sip from her glass, fear filling her eyes. 'You know what thirteen means, don't you?'

CHAPTER 8

2005

Ava had lent Lena a pair of high heels that she'd been coveting for ages. They had the same size feet, only Lena's were wider, and the shoes pinched at the sides. 'Sod this,' she said, and put her trainers on, slipping the party shoes into a plastic bag. 'I'll change once we get there.' Excitement mixed with the buzz of the alcohol made her fizz like a sparkler. 'Let's stop off in the park for a cigarette,' she added. 'Calm my nerves.'

Ava was giddy at the thought of the night ahead too, until she thought about Gareth, and then her mood dipped.

Danny's house backed onto the park, and they could hear the music from the bench they were sitting on. Lena blew out smoke and hummed along. 'I knew Danny would have some good tunes,' she said.

Ava's phone buzzed in her pocket, and she took it out and read the text.

'Who is it?'

She pulled a face.

'Gareth,' Lena said, and they both laughed, though Ava's giggle was followed by a surge of dread.

Lena pulled the fur jacket around her shoulders. She'd borrowed that from Ava too; it looked good over her short leather skirt and bright pink top. Ava looked at her friend and couldn't help feeling envious of the curves she was developing. She herself was like a pole, straight up, straight down. The red dress she was wearing looked better on the hanger.

'At least I know for sure what I have to do,' she said. 'I'm going to tell Gareth we're over as soon as I get there.' She tried to ignore the sinking feeling that she might have to leave the country before he'd forget about her.

'After a stiff drink, that is. You haven't had half as much as I have.'

'I'm not used to it, that's why.'

Lena didn't say out loud that she'd watched her father often enough. She pulled a bottle of martini out of the carrier bag. 'Here.' She unscrewed the cap. 'It's better with lemonade, but it'll do the trick for now.'

Ava took a sip and shuddered. 'It tastes sickly on its own,' she said. 'You know, my parents would actually kill me if they could see me now. What if there was an emergency and they came back and didn't know where I was?'

'That is so not going to happen. Why do you worry about everything? You don't know what real worry is.' Lena took a swig from the bottle, savouring the sting.

Ava was watching Danny's house. The music had got louder, and laughter pealed out, voices shouting. What if the neighbours reported them and she got caught by the police? Her imagination always ran away across fields and over stiles, envisaging the worst. One of her parents being taken ill and having to rush home, or a broken-down car, an accident.

Lena clicked her fingers. 'You're doing it again. What catastrophic scenario are you conjuring up this time?' She was always able to read her best friend's mind.

Ava laughed. 'You know me so well. Seriously, though, you must think I'm a right princess. Your life is way harder and you never go on about it.'

Lena shrugged.

'You can, you know. Talk to me, I mean. About your mum and stuff.'

Both girls were staring at the house, where some boys had come out into the garden and started play-fighting.

'Boys are such kids,' Lena said. 'My brother's like that.'

A silence grew between them. Ava waited for her to say more. Lena never talked much about her brother. At last she cleared her throat.

'He's twenty-three, can't stop getting into trouble. That's how come he's in prison. He stole a car and took it for a joyride. Then he did it again, and again. Got caught every time. Idiot. You'd think he'd have learned his lesson the first time. Now I'm stuck with Dad. You're lucky having parents who would go mad knowing you were out tonight. My dad couldn't care less, as long as I'm home to cook his dinner. As soon as I'm sixteen, I'll be off. Let them sort themselves out. I've had enough.'

At her friend's words Ava resolved to have a chat with her mother, try to get her to change her mind about Lena. She must know about Lena's brother; that had to be the reason she wasn't keen on her. Ava's family were always exchanging knowing looks, excluding her, when it came to Lena. But if her mum knew how hard her home life was, she'd have more compassion. Mum was a caring person. Too caring. Ava shuddered, thinking again about how much trouble she would be in if her parents found out about tonight.

She shoved aside her worries and hugged her friend. The glitter on her chest shimmered, and when they pulled apart, Lena's dress was glittery too.

'You've got me,' Ava said. 'I'll stick by you. Forever.' No boy was important enough to come between them.

CHAPTER 9

Ava

'Put it out of sight,' I tell Lena. Thirteen is unlucky; how could she not know that?

She slams the fridge door.

'What does it mean?' I ask.

'I don't know. I mean, thirteen can only refer to one thing, but I have no idea who sent it.' Her dark eyes are anxious. 'Look, it's going to be hard to forget about it, but there's nothing we can do now. I promise you we'll talk about it later, but for now, I just want you to have a good time. Will you try?'

I nod, because I have no choice, and she hugs me. We go back into the lounge. The raucous sound of laughter is heard from the street, and footsteps head down the front path. Panic is whirling inside me. I pick up my drink. Voices filter in from the entrance hall, and the work crowd troop in shouting, 'Surprise!' each of them carrying a silver balloon. There are a few people with them I don't recognise; their partners presumably. They release the shiny helium balloons, which drift up to the ceiling, and Steph gives me a wave. *You can do this.*

'Drinks over here!' Lena says. She hands out bottles, ladles punch into glasses. Steph opts for orange juice. The chatter gives me time to compose myself. A couple of the guys are carrying boxes, which Lena tells them to leave by the back door. I go over to the group and am hugged by everyone. Introductions are made, conversation continues and the atmosphere in the room gets even livelier. Someone turns the volume up on the music.

Steph is in a vintage fifties dress and looks fabulous. Her boyfriend Felix is wearing a tweed cap and a checked jacket with blue trousers and loafers. They both come over as soon as they've got their drinks. Steph gives me a hug. 'You look beautiful,' she says in my ear, and I squeeze her tight. 'So classy, with your swan-like neck. And your dress is amazing. Is this the one Ben sent you?'

I nod. Would she think I was classy if she could see the ugly scar I'm hiding? My guilt is gouged in deep; no amount of rubbing my shoulder gets rid of it, but I can't help trying.

'Hi, Felix. What's with all the boxes?'

'A little present from the office. They wanted to celebrate your leaving in style, seeing as how you wouldn't let them organise a do at work.'

'I can't bear any more suspense. What is it?'

'I'm not sure I'm allowed to say yet.' He looks around the room. 'Hey, Lena, can I tell her what's in the boxes yet?'

Lena is fussing around at the food table, putting glasses on a tray. 'I suppose so …'

Felix grins. 'It's fireworks.'

'I'll never forget your reaction that time we went to see them at Ally Pally,' Steph says. 'I've told Felix all about it.'

He nods. 'I'm the same, love 'em.'

'You were like a little kid looking on in wonder. And because it's Bonfire Night, we thought we'd have a mini display here.'

Excitement whirls in my stomach and I clap my hands. 'Amazing,' I say. I remember watching the colours exploding into the cold air filled with the visible puffs of breath from the eager crowd, heads leaning back as they gazed up at the November sky – it was magical. This must be the surprise Lena referred to earlier. 'But won't it be dangerous?' I ask, thinking of what could go wrong, what accidents could happen.

'Of course not,' Felix says. 'I'm in charge, so you don't need to worry. If you can't trust a fireman to do it, then who can you trust?' We all laugh. 'We'll set it up a bit later and let everyone know when it's happening.' He takes a glass of punch from the tray that Lena is carrying around, and winces as he takes a sip. 'God, that's strong.'

'You didn't bring the car, did you?' I ask.

'Unfortunately I lost the toss, so I'm driving,' Steph says. 'So, did you guess about the party?'

'I've known for ages. Lena is rubbish at hiding stuff from me – I don't think she's ever managed to keep a secret. But I only told her I knew yesterday.'

'I bet she was gutted you'd found out.'

'She was more relieved, to be honest. That way I could help her with all the preparations today. It will be sad to leave this place.'

'When are you moving out?'

'Tomorrow, though Lena hasn't done any packing. She's left it all to the last minute, as usual.'

'She's not your responsibility, I've told you that before. Just relax and enjoy yourself. The house looks lovely, by the way.'

'It's a great place,' Felix says. 'I'm surprised Lena wants to leave. Can't she get someone else to move in? I would have thought she'd get loads of interest.'

'I know, that's exactly what I said. But she says she doesn't want to stay without me.'

'Well of course not, who would?' says Felix, and we all laugh. He drains his glass. 'Time for another drink. Can I get either of you anything?'

'No thanks,' we both say.

As Felix moves away, Steph gives me a knowing look. 'That's not the main reason why Lena doesn't want to get anyone in, is it?' she asks.

Steph and I have grown close since she joined the charity two years ago as a fellow fund-raiser, and I've opened up to her a lot over the course of our friendship. She thinks Lena's too dependent on me – that's what she's getting at. That Lena would refuse to share with anyone else but she doesn't understand the complicated dynamics of our relationship, all the history. And how could she, when I can never explain?

'It's going to be hard for me too,' I say. 'She's been fabulous these past few weeks, looking after me when I wasn't feeling great, with all the stuff going on at work. And she makes me laugh so much. We've lived together since we were sixteen.' We're both watching Lena as we chat, the way she's so at ease with people as she moves in and out of the groups that are forming, checking to see if everyone has enough to drink, complimenting guests on their outfits. The doorbell rings again, and she disappears out of the room.

The girls from work come across, and I sip at a glass of punch and try to relax. The beat of the music is insistent and loud, and we're almost shouting at each other over it. Sophie is telling me about a funny incident that happened in the office this week. It's weird to think I won't be going back there. I push aside the thought and enjoy the delicious ripple of excitement that shimmies through me whenever I think about New York.

Felix comes back and slings his arm around Steph. 'Great music,' he says. 'Are you sure I can't get you ladies anything else before I go and chat football with my buddies?'

Steph laughs. 'You go. I want Ava all to myself. We've got my Christmas shopping trip to New York to discuss.'

A smile spreads over my face. 'I still can't believe it's real. Ben's been asking me to go over for so long.'

'I'd have jumped at the chance ages ago. Though you know we're going to be lost without you in the office, don't you? Who's going to organise all the social events, the collections, everything basically?'

'You'll manage. I'm going to miss you all too.' Her words warm me inside. 'Who else from work is coming?' I ask.

'Pretty much everyone.'

'Not *everyone*, I hope?'

Steph gives me a look. 'Yes, I'm afraid so. Lena issued a general invitation.'

'Surely not Pete?'

She nods, her cheeks glowing. 'I tried to tell the others the invitation wasn't meant for him, that you wouldn't want him there, but it was too late, someone had already emailed it around. Maybe he wants to apologise.'

My heart drums inside me, in time with the pounding music. The last person I want to see is Pete. It's bad enough that Gareth will be here. His devotion is another thing I most definitely will not miss. I wish I could transport myself into next week and be strolling through Central Park with Ben, marvelling at the vast space filled with lush greenery tucked away amongst so much concrete. But the mention of Pete erases the excitement that has been flickering on and off all day. The one good thing about leaving work is getting away from him. I never want to see him again. The last few months have been hard, but he made it easier for me to make a decision, finally giving in to Ben's pleas.

'You don't have to speak to him,' Steph says. 'And anyway, he might not even come.'

'He will come.' We both know Pete. Any excuse for a free drink, a bit of banter with his team. 'Team building,' we say in unison. It's an in-joke, but it isn't really funny; nothing about Pete is funny any more.

'Look,' she says. 'It's your party, everyone is here for you. Nobody will let him do or say anything inappropriate.'

It's sweet of her to say it, but I know it's meaningless. They all still have to work with him. He's the boss; nobody is going to stand up to him. But I don't say this out loud, sipping at my drink instead and savouring the burn.

CHAPTER 10

Lena

More people have arrived and Felix has gone outside with a couple of friends to light a bonfire. A fireworks display has started somewhere nearby and the dark sky is lit up with vibrant bursts of colour and loud popping noises. I wander around with a bottle of wine, filling up people's glasses.

Ava follows me into the kitchen.

'Come outside,' she says, leading me into the garden. 'That way we can talk privately. You won't believe it – they've invited Pete. Did you know?'

'No way. I sent the invitation to the office, but I thought it was obvious they weren't to invite him. It was Steph I sent the invitation to. Do you want me to speak to her?'

'No! Pete's an irritation, but that's not what I want to talk about. I'm still wondering about that cake.'

The bonfire is lit, illuminating the shadows of the garden. I smile over at Felix, one hand on Ava's back as we cross over to the bench at the end of the garden. The fire crackles and spits and the noise covers our conversation.

'It's shaken me up,' she says, taking a hasty swig of her drink.

'You're doing great,' I say. 'Nobody would know what just happened back there.'

'What did happen? What does it mean?'

I shrug. 'I don't know. Have you any idea who might have sent it? Has anything else happened?'

She shakes her head, watching the fire, and I can see the reflection of the flames flickering in her eyes. Her jaw moves, and I sense she's not telling me everything.

'Talk to me. What's going on?'

'I don't know.' Now she looks at me, determination in her gaze. 'I'm leaving the country in two days, so I'm not going to let receiving a cake from some freak bother me. Like you said earlier, this is my party and I'm going to enjoy myself. Everyone from work has been so supportive, and I'm not going to let the threat of Pete coming spoil things either.'

'That's more like it. But I don't expect him to show up. He wasn't meant to be invited.'

'I'll just avoid him if he does. Steph doesn't think it will be a problem.' She smiles wryly, watching the dancing flames, smoke filling the air. 'I didn't realise until I took a step back and had a good look at myself how much I did at that place. I'm confident I'll be able to find a similar job in the States.'

'It makes it so real when you say things like that. Are you sure you don't want to wait until you've secured a job? You know I don't want you to go.'

'Getting away from here is probably the best thing I can do right now,' she says.

A stray spark jumps from the fire and lands on my leg.

'Ouch.' I jump to my feet. But it's a fleeting moment of pain, and anyway, that's not what's really hurting me.

'Ava,' Felix calls, and she gets up and walks over to the bonfire. The metallic blue of her dress flashes in the glow of the firelight, and a stitch-like pain digs into my side. Does she realise how much her leaving pains me? My hand wanders to the strip of plaster that covers my tattoo. It's been healed for a while now, but I'm waiting for the right moment to reveal it. The day Ava told me she'd finally made up her mind that she was going to live with Ben was the day I came up with the design. It's a special one. And Ava will be the first to see it. It's for her, after all.

The wind blows across the garden, causing the fire to whoosh and leap, and I feel cold all over. I walk quickly back into the house and pour myself a large glass of gin, no mixer, noting the chip in the glass, another flaw at this party that I wanted so desperately to be perfect.

'Doorbell!' a man says, and I'm relieved to have something to do. I leave my glass on the side and go back to the hall, adjusting the volume on the music as I pass. There's too much talking; nobody's dancing yet. I open the door, but I don't recognise the man who stands in front of me. He holds out a bag containing some bottles that clink against one another. A quick glance tells me it's craft beer, vibrant-coloured labels on fancy bottles.

'Nice,' I say. 'I'm Lena, by the way. I take it I've invited you and you're not just some random guy walking past the hottest party in town.'

He's big, but muscly, like he works out, the kind of guy who has a high bar to do pull-ups on in the doorway of his bedroom. The kind of guy I go for. His hair is dark and curly and his chestnut-brown eyes appear to be laughing at me.

'Good to meet you, Lena.'

'And you are …?'

'Pete,' he says. 'I'm Ava's boss. I expect she's told you about me.'

He looks nothing like the picture I have in my imagination, and I fix a smile on my face.

'Pete, hi. I know who you are.'

'I've brought some fireworks; they're in my car boot. Is Steph around? She said I need to give them to Felix. I presume they're both here already.'

'Yeah, he's been building the bonfire out back. I'll let him know you're here.'

He follows me into the living room. Someone calls Felix in from outside, and he takes Pete's car keys.

'Want me to come and help?' Pete asks him.

'No need, mate, I've got this. This is Lena, have you two met? She's organised a pretty amazing party. There's enough booze to last the weekend, I reckon.'

'I'll get you a drink,' I say. 'What would you like?'

'Beer, please, one of these is fine. Help yourself to one too.' He indicates the bag.

Steph watches me as I go over to the table and put the bottles down, pouring one out for Pete and one for myself. I've had enough punch for now. The glass feels as cold as my hands. More people are arriving and I don't know who they are, but I don't care by this point. The party is buzzing and that's all that matters.

'Cheers,' Pete says, studying my face intently. His eyes are pale brown, light to my dark ones. *Opposites attract.* His muscles flex as he moves. I'm not what you'd call a gym bunny, but I know a good body when I see one. With those biceps and his height, he could pick me up and throw me over his shoulder. Then I remember how he treated Ava and feel a twinge of guilt. Deep breaths, Lena. This party isn't going to be spoilt by an idiot like him.

'I don't suppose I can smoke in here?'

'You suppose right. In the garden.' I indicate the back door with my head, my eyes resting on his for a moment.

'Join me?' he asks, producing a packet of cigarettes from his pocket. His hand partially covers the label, and I catch a glimpse of the words ... *seriously harms you and others around you.*

Ava's eyes are flashing a warning across the room, taking me back to the desperate feeling I had that evening when she told me what had happened. So what if he's fit on the outside? I know what lurks underneath that muscle-bound exterior. She must know she's got nothing to worry about. I'm just keen to get the measure of him. Hopefully the smile I send her is reassuring as I follow him outside and across the lawn.

'I didn't have you down as a smoker,' I say. 'Obviously you're into fitness.'

'Do you work out, Lena?'

I laugh. 'If you call running for the bus working out, then yes.'

'Cigarette?'

'Go on. I could do with one, actually.' Despite having given up years ago, the craving has returned tonight.

'It must be hard for you, Ava moving away. You've known her a long time, haven't you? She's talked about you. I bet she's talked about me too,' he says, smoke spooling out of his mouth, twisting through the air as he speaks.

'Yeah, she has.' His tone sends an uncomfortable sensation to my stomach and the tobacco tastes foul on my tongue. Why am I even bothering with this guy? I grind the cigarette under my heel until it disintegrates. My legs feel cold. 'Time to go, things to do,' I say.

'Catch you later,' he says. I can feel his eyes boring into me as I walk away, my shoulders stiffening in response.

'What were you talking to Pete about?' Steph asks, blocking my way into the kitchen.

'Nothing much,' I say. 'Just having a cigarette.'

She pulls a face.

'I didn't want to really, but I am the host and I was just being polite. I don't want any trouble for Ava. Let's hope he stays out there.'

'Why did you invite him?' she says.

'I didn't. I thought it was obvious that he wasn't included in the open invitation. I assumed you must have told him about it.'

'I certainly didn't. Somebody else emailed it to all staff before I could warn them.'

'Surely no one in your office would have done that; they all know about him and Ava.'

'Maybe he overheard us talking about it. It's hard to exclude him when everyone else is invited.'

'I don't want him upsetting Ava,' I say. 'This party has to be perfect.'

'I'm hoping the reason he's here is to make amends. I know he's not happy that Ava is leaving. She's the most experienced member of our team and she's so good at rallying us all. You know what she's like, such a sunny disposition. We're all gutted.'

The music changes.

'Oh, I love this song,' Steph says. 'Ava tells me you've lots of surprises planned. I think she's a bit nervous.'

'She needn't be. Actually, you could help me with something.' I check that Ava is nowhere within earshot, but she's unwrapping a present on the other side of the room, silver paper catching the light and twinkling along with the fairy lights. 'We've got a special firework saved for midnight, which Felix has got in hand, but just before that, I'd like to cut the cake and I thought it would be lovely if Ava would perform for us. You know she's recently started playing the piano again, and she's written a piece.'

Steph claps her hand together. 'That's a fabulous idea.'

'Do you think she'll go for it?'

'Oh yes. She told me once that playing an instrument is far easier for her than talking about her feelings.'

It used to fascinate me how Ava could sit and practise the piano for hours, lost in her own world. Sit me down for even five minutes with a book and I can't keep still.

Steph continues. 'She said that having an audience validates her, as she can give pleasure to others too.' She looks over at Ava. 'And who knows when she'll get to play her own piano again.'

The first time I heard Ava play was at school. She'd disappeared one lunchtime and I was looking for her everywhere. Out in the playground, in the gym, even in the library, although since we'd been hanging out together, she didn't need to hide there any more.

We healed each other's loneliness. A teacher pointed me in the direction of the music practice area, and the tinkling notes lured me to the end room, where Ava was playing with her back to the door, immediately recognisable by her elegant posture and long blonde hair in a plait. It was a complicated-sounding classical tune, not the sort of thing I knew anything about, but watching her fingers flying across the keys made little bumps pop all over my skin. The same tingling sensation reappears now just thinking about it, and I feel an overwhelming urge to cry.

CHAPTER 11

2005

Outside Danny's house, Ava checked her phone while Lena struggled out of her trainers and slipped on her party shoes. Gareth had sent a message.

Are you there yet?

She scowled and deleted the text.

Lena stashed her trainers behind a large fern in a weathered earthenware pot. Ava was about to ring the bell, but the front door was already open, and Lena barged straight in. The hallway was empty, and they followed the sound of the music to the kitchen.

'I'd get lost if I lived here,' Lena said.

Ava nodded, but the house was similar in size to her own. Lena's flat, in comparison, consisted of a dark, narrow corridor with a handful of tiny rooms leading off it. Just the hallway here was twice as big as her cramped kitchen.

Ava checked her dress in the mirror and adjusted the straps. She wished she didn't look so worried. She'd get this matter with Gareth sorted, then start enjoying herself.

'There's Danny,' Lena said under her breath before going straight over to him, exaggerating the swing of her hips in her tight skirt, heels wobbling beneath her.

'Hey, Danny.'

'Hey, Lena, Ava. How's it going?'

'We've brought goodies.' Lena waved the carrier bag at him.

'Cool. Stick it in the kitchen and help yourselves to a drink. Joe has made a lethal punch – I'd definitely recommend it.'

'Follow me, girls,' Joe said.

Lena nudged Ava knowingly, but Joe had long hair and John Lennon glasses and wasn't her type at all. He looked as if he listened to old hippy music and played a guitar. He was the sort of guy Martha went for. Guilt surfaced the instant she thought about her sister, who would never lie to their parents about where she was going. But she dismissed the thought. Martha and her parents were hundreds of miles away. Joe ladled some bright red punch into two large plastic glasses, dragging her away from her thoughts, before going back to his friends.

'Let's have a look round,' Lena said, tugging Ava's arm. She leaned in so close, Ava nearly choked on her Chloé perfume, the floral scent making her cough. 'I want to see the bedrooms,' she whispered into Ava's ear.

Ava experienced the usual mix of emotions Lena made her feel. Her best friend always led her along a dangerous path – it was scary, but just so flipping exciting.

A group of girls from school wearing baby-doll tops in bright colours and figure-hugging skirts stood on one side of the room, giggling and sending coy glances over to the boys. Lena waved at them and they acted as if they hadn't seen her.

'Losers,' she said under her breath.

She led Ava back through the hall and up the stairs. The soft pale blue carpet was tricky to negotiate in heels. There were four bedrooms; the first one had coats all over the bed, and Lena shrugged off her fur jacket and waited for Ava to dump her coat too before marching out of the room, her friend following in her wake. The master bedroom was at the front of the house, and she headed straight for it.

'You can't go in there,' Ava said, looking down the wide staircase.

'Why not? You're such a scaredy cat. I'm not going to touch anything. Just want to see how the other half live.'

Ava was struck by guilt again. She didn't like to think of being in Mr and Mrs Seymour's bedroom. Her mum would have been furious if Ava's friends had ever gone into hers.

'I'm waiting here,' she said, standing up to her friend for once. 'Hurry up.'

Her phone buzzed. Gareth again. And again.

Wish we'd gone together.

Are you there yet?

What are you wearing?

I'm on my way.

Lena emerged from the bedroom rubbing a lavender-smelling cream into her hands.

'It's like a chemist in there, lotions and potions everywhere. How many creams does one woman need? I smell expensive now, like a supermodel. Danny won't be able to resist me,' she said with a laugh, fluttering her eyelashes.

Ava was still looking at her phone. 'Gareth's seriously getting on my nerves. Having a boyfriend is meant to be fun, isn't it? Mind you, he's the only boy who's ever shown any interest in me.'

'Ava, loads of boys are going to go for you. You're gorgeous; you look like a model.'

'Yeah, but I'm not like you, I find it hard to talk to boys. My face goes bright red and my throat seizes up.'

'Follow me, babe. I'll show you how it's done.' Lena squeezed her arm. 'Me and you …'

Ava grinned and joined her in finishing the sentence. '… against the world.'

CHAPTER 12

Ava

Felix is down at the far end of the garden, watching the fire, his face glowing in the heat. He grins when he sees me.

'Not bad, is it? As long as the rain holds off, it should last us for the evening.'

'When did you do all this?' I ask, looking at the mound of wood piled against the tree.

He stands up and stretches his back. 'You've got Lena to thank for most of it. One of your neighbours provided the wood.' The sound of crackling fills the air. 'Right,' he says. 'I'll just nip out to the car and get the potatoes.'

'Potatoes?'

'Lena wanted a traditional firework party like people used to have, and Steph offered to organise jacket potatoes. She prepared them all at home and they're wrapped in foil and ready to go. Food will be done by about eleven, and we'll have the fireworks ready for midnight. We're good to go now that the rest of them have arrived.'

'You've had them delivered?'

'Your boss brought them; he paid for the whole lot. Said it was the least he could do.'

'Pete?' Despite the heat from the fire, I shiver. Maybe it's his way of apologising.

The flames flicker high into the sky and fireworks erupt in the distance. A dog barks loudly, as if sending out a warning. The burning smell fills my senses and transports me back to a holiday cottage in Devon my parents used to take us to, Mum tearing up paper to throw on the fire, chunks of coal glowing with white heat; Martha and I daring each other to touch the fireguard with tiny fingers, my sister pulling my hands away at the last minute, protecting me. I allow myself the thought that I can't bring myself to voice. Is it Martha who has been tormenting me over the years? Surely she wouldn't let her resentment towards Lena go that far? Not with her blossoming career. Does she still see Lena as a usurper, taking over her sisterly role? But if it is her, what is she trying to tell me?

'Earth to Ava,' Felix says, making me jump. He points to Steph, who is waving at me from the back door.

On my way through to the lounge, I grab a plastic glass and fill it with punch, which most people seem to be avoiding, probably due to the sheer amount of rum Lena threw in. It mixes with the wine I had earlier and my mind feels looser, more relaxed.

Steph leads me over to two women, one of them my friend Esther from the gym, who gives me a beautifully wrapped present but makes me promise to open it later. The other woman Steph introduces as Kate, the girlfriend of a guy from Accounts. Her black hair is shaped in a striking Cleopatra cut, and she's wearing a dark jumpsuit with chunky lace-up boots. She apologises for not having brought me anything, and I tell her I didn't expect gifts. She goes off to get a drink, and more friends who have just arrived come over to greet me. The room is full of people now, and heat bounces off the walls, making my back feel prickly with sweat. Some of the work crowd start dancing – it's that kind of music. There's a brilliant vibe in the air and I'm just thinking how well it's going when Steph takes me to one side and tells me Pete has arrived.

'Lena let him in,' she says.

The room, which moments earlier felt too hot, feels suddenly chilly. Even though I'd been warned I'd been hoping he wouldn't turn up.

'You OK?' she asks, and rubs my arm.

'Just wishing he hadn't come, that's all.'

'He's your ex-boss, remember. After tonight, you can forget him. You don't need to speak to him, and definitely not on your own. I'm sure he'll stick with the other guys from work. I can't imagine he'd want to be alone with you either.'

I nod. 'You're right.'

'Of course I'm right. Why don't we go and dance and you can shake him out of your system?'

I laugh. 'No, you go, I'm going to go and chat with my friends over there.'

'OK.' She goes off to dance and I wander into the kitchen, where I pretend to listen to one of my friends telling me about his new job, but it's hard to concentrate knowing Pete is here, in this house. I've half an ear on the conversation, but I can't help remembering, with a shudder, the day everything changed.

It was a Friday. Pete had given everyone else the afternoon off, but I had to stay to finish a funding bid I was helping him with, as the deadline was five o'clock that afternoon. I didn't mind, thrilled to be working on such an important project.

Pete seemed like the perfect boss. He'd only recently started at the charity, and had taken the staff out for drinks to get to know us. When he had selected me for his first team, I'd been flattered. I was good at my job and he recognised that. During our regular work drinks in the pub on Fridays, we got on well, conversation flowing between us, and I liked the direction in which he was planning on taking the organisation.

'Hey, Ava,' he said. 'Just you and me left holding the fort today.' The grin on his face showed he was happy with the situation, but I didn't think anything of it.

We made our deadline and I was taking my bag out of my drawer, looking forward to my regular Friday night Skype with Ben, when Pete came out of his office holding a bottle of whisky and two glasses. I continued putting my coat on as he set everything down on the filing cabinet.

'Don't rush off. I want to thank you for working so hard on this bid.'

'It's my job, no need to thank me. A drink would be lovely some other time, but I have plans tonight.'

'Come on,' Pete said. 'Just a quick one.'

'I'm sorry, I can't stay.'

'What plans exactly?'

'Ben and I have a regular Skype at this time, and it's during his break at work so I can't be late.'

He stepped closer. 'It must be difficult with your boyfriend living miles away. That can't be much of a relationship.' He poured a generous amount of whisky into both glasses. I pulled my coat around myself, secured the belt with fingers that weren't entirely steady. He stepped towards me, forcing me to fall back, then leaned across me and placed his left hand on the wall behind me. With his right hand he touched my face, and I jerked away.

'No. What are you doing?' He was so close I could smell coffee and stale cigarette smoke on his breath, and for one terrible moment I thought he was going to kiss me, but he must have seen the revulsion on my face because he dropped his arm and stepped back.

'Bloody tease,' he said. 'You've been flirting with me for weeks.'

I ran out of the office, my pulse pounding with adrenalin, unable to believe what had happened. It was the push I needed. I wrote out my resignation letter that evening and spent two hours on the phone to Ben, telling him everything. Well, almost everything. As we discussed starting a new life together in New York, his excitement pulsed down the phone line.

Ben had been asking me to come and live in the States for years. It started after university. Once he'd finished his degree, he had to return to America; he'd secured a position working for a bank in New York, and it was too good an opportunity to miss. I'd resisted for so long because I couldn't leave Lena behind after everything she'd done for me. How Lena and I felt about each other was how I imagine twins must feel. But circumstances had changed and it was time we became less bound up with one another. It's hard for her to accept, as she's the one being left behind, but Ben is my future, and she has to move on.

The kitchen is empty now save for Kate, who I was introduced to earlier. She's filling a small plate with biscuits, cheese, gherkins and tiny rolled-up stuffed vine leaves. She smiles at me before heading off into the garden. Steph dances in from the other room, leaning against the counter and holding her side.

'I'm exhausted,' she says. 'It's been ages since I had a good dance. Remember that club we used to go to over in Highgate? We'd spend hours on the dance floor without even stopping for a drink. I don't know where I used to get the energy from to stay up all night.'

We both laugh.

'It's a brilliant party, just listen,' she says. We're quiet for a moment, hear the house vibrating with the thumping music and the loud chatter and laughter that mingles in the air. 'What are you drinking?'

I look around for my glass. 'Punch, but there's only so much of it I can cope with.'

Steph laughs. 'I agree. Gin and tonic for madam?'

'Great.' I smile at her. 'I'm so glad you're here. I wonder what time Ben will arrive.' I go to check my phone before remembering that I can't find it. I guess he'll assume I'm busy with the party. He knows I'm not the kind of person who's sticking photos on Instagram every minute.

'Lena was telling me you've written a piece recently.' Steph mixes some tonic into my drink.

My cheeks flush. 'It's nothing special, just something I'm working on.' I've been surprised at how easily composing has come back to me, and how much I have to say. 'Maybe we could hear it later?'

'Oh no, who would want to hear me play the piano?'

'I think your friends would very much like it. I know I would. What I don't understand is why you ever stopped.'

I take the glass she's offering me, hoping she doesn't see the flush that rushes to my cheeks, my fingers stiffening like they used to when I tried to play. Steph has become a good friend and I'd love to be able to tell her the real reason my mind and body froze whenever I sat down to play. If I hadn't been invited to that assembly …

'Too busy, I guess,' I say lamely.

'Actually,' Steph says, 'I rather think Lena might be hoping you'll play for us.'

'Really?' My face feels even hotter.

'Please don't say anything. I don't want to spoil her surprise, but I thought I'd better check you don't hate the idea.'

I chew at my lip, considering, wiggling my fingers against my thigh.

'No, I'm flattered.' Ben has never heard me play, which makes me want him to be here this evening more than ever, but I don't want to jinx it by saying it out loud. Dad must have known Lena wanted me to play. I wondered why he insisted on waiting until tomorrow to move the piano.

'Shall we go back in and dance?' Steph says.

I nod, following her through to the living room, which is a heaving mass of sweating bodies, glistening foreheads, waving arms and raised glasses. Friends who haven't spoken to me yet come over, and I'm feeling much more relaxed. Chatting about my plans make it feel even more real, and the music and the alcohol are making me tingle with excitement.

After a while, sweat is trickling down my back and I decide I need fresh air. I check the garden but can't see any sign of Pete. An image flashes before me: Pete's face close enough for me to smell the tobacco on his breath. I gag, tasting the punch. I've had enough alcohol; time for something refreshing. Without thinking, I open the fridge, only to be confronted by the black cake, the number 13 glaring out at me. I rub my arms, and it's not the fridge that's making me feel cold.

'That's an interesting cake.' Fiona's voice makes me jump, and I slam the door so hard the fridge vibrates. She visibly recoils. 'You look like a ghost. Are you OK? Here,' she pulls out a chair, 'sit down.' She fusses around the table until she locates a bottle of sparkling water, and pours me a glass, sitting opposite me. 'Are you feeling overwhelmed?'

'Something like that. That weird cake was delivered earlier and I don't know who sent it.' As I recount what happened, I'm aware how ridiculous it sounds and the panicked fluttering in my chest slows down. Fiona tidies up glasses and plates of food debris on the table as I'm talking.

'The card will have fallen off, that's all. Make sure you're not the first to sample it. I heard your creepy boss was here. Let him have the first slice.'

We both laugh, and I drink some water.

'That's more like it. Do you fancy something alcoholic now?' She wrinkles her nose at the punch, which is down to mostly fruit, and holds up a bottle of gin.

'No, water's fine, but you go ahead.'

'I'm not drinking, actually.' She rubs the label on the bottle and her face flushes red. My eyes flicker to her lap, where her cardigan covers a slight bump.

'Oh my God, you're pregnant, aren't you?'

A huge smile lights up her face and her cheeks glow.

'I'm so happy for you. Is it a boy or a girl?'

'A surprise. I don't want to know. Malcolm wants a boy. He's probably right. Teenage girls are so troublesome, aren't they?'

A flash of red springs into my mind, angry words hurled from a girl in a sparkly dress.

'Congratulations,' I say.

'And to you too.'

'I hope I'm doing the right thing.'

'What makes you say that? You've been talking about it for years.'

I rub at an invisible spot on my knee. 'I feel terrible about leaving Lena behind.'

Fiona's face crumples into a frown. 'She'll be fine. Lena's a tough cookie. She's always known how to look after herself.'

I rub even harder at my knee. 'I know it used to annoy you when she was always coming up to Cambridge, but she was only looking out for me; that's why I'm so indebted to her. She was a huge support when I was going through a difficult time.'

'I suspected as much. I wanted to support you too, but I could see you didn't want to talk about it.' She puts her hand over mine to stop me worrying at my tights. Instinctively I move my hand to my shoulder. 'You didn't go and see the student counsellor for fun. You're lucky to have such a devoted friend. With Skype, you'll never be far apart. You and Ben are still going strong after years of practice.'

'It feels disloyal after she's given me so much help. Now that I'm fine, I'm flitting off and abandoning her.'

'Even more reason for her to be thrilled at the way you've blossomed. You're spreading your wings. If you love someone, you're meant to let them go, everyone knows that. I bet you anything you're worrying unnecessarily.'

A cold draught blows in through the open door, and I shiver. The music in the other room ramps up in volume. I hope Fiona is right.

CHAPTER 13

Lena

The hall is empty, everyone stuffed into the living room. Someone is messing with the music, keeps turning it up and down. The volume surges again as I open the door to see a bulky figure with his back to me. Gareth. He's got on the battered leather jacket he's been wearing ever since I can remember. He hitches his faded jeans up in a familiar gesture.

'Gareth.'

He turns around, clutching something to his chest. I assume it's a bottle of wine, until he steps forward. It's a rose.

'For me?' I'm joking – I know it's for Ava. No other girl exists for Gareth; it's been that way since school, when he used to gaze at her from behind his history textbook. 'You're late. That's not like you.' Give him a chance to see Ava, and he's usually the first to arrive.

'I had to work late. Are you going to let me in?'

'Of course. Come and have some of my delicious punch.' I know he won't; safe, predictable Gareth is strictly a beer man.

'No thanks. I've brought some cans.' He hands me a carrier bag.

'Drinks are in the kitchen.' I lead him through the dark hallway.

'Where's Ava? I want to give her this.' Up close, I notice the rose is black, the stem wrapped in tin foil.

'Did you drop one of those round earlier? Someone left something similar outside.'

'Not me. I've been at work.'

I open kitchen cupboards, slamming each door as I'm confronted with empty spaces. The slender crystal vase I'm looking for is Ava's and it's gone. Of course it is.

'It's a bit empty in here, isn't it?' Gareth asks.

'Too right it is.' I give up looking and rinse out an empty wine bottle, half filling it with water. 'Here, give me that.'

Gareth hands over the rose before moving to the window. He's spotted Ava.

'Who's she with?' He's practically pressing his nose against the glass.

I glance outside, where Ava is chatting to Felix, her face lit up by the fire he's started. Gareth hitches his trousers up again, and his jaw tightens.

'He's the partner of someone she works with. Honestly, Gareth, there's no point getting jealous. She's engaged to Ben, remember.'

'That won't last.' He takes a long drink from his can. 'Living together won't be easy after all this time apart, and she'll be homesick. Remember how she was at university. She needed you, still does in my opinion. She also needs a man who can be around to look after her.'

'What, like you, you mean? Give it up, Gareth. It was years ago that you went out with her.' His shoulders stiffen and I soften my voice. 'I know it's hard when you like someone, but ...' It has to be said.

He shuffles around, looking down at his scruffy trainers. 'She hasn't told you, has she?'

'Told me what?'

He continues watching Ava in the garden, his gaze intent. Smoke is now billowing up into the sky, and the smell filters through the open doors. There's a strange smirk on his face, and I wonder if he's been drinking on his way over. He's not usually like this.

'Obviously she doesn't share everything with you, otherwise she'd have told you about us.'

'When you were in sixth form?' I laugh out loud. 'Seriously?'

'That's not what I mean. I'm talking about now.'

'What? She's engaged to Ben.'

'Where is he then?'

'He's on his way, he's been delayed – but keep that to yourself, it's a surprise.'

'You don't see it even if it's going on right under your nose. Something happened with me and Ava. The other week, when you'd gone to bed, remember?'

'Ye-es.' I was shattered that night, on my feet at work from eight till ten covering a shift, making conversation with clients, running around after useless juniors. Ava insisted I accompany her, as she always did when Gareth invited her out for a drink. 'Just one,' she promised. Three pints at the pub, Ava drunk, unusually so for her, and I hadn't the energy to stop him inviting himself in for coffee. I left them to it, sitting on the sofa. Ava was different that night, it's true, but I didn't think anything of it at the time.

'I stayed over,' he says. 'I woke really early, left before you got up.'

I'm rapidly recalling the next morning. I had a day off, and I always sleep in when I get the chance. A sick feeling churns in my stomach.

Gareth's lips twitch. 'Ben needs to know, so it's good to hear he's on his way. Ava likes to spring surprises on people at parties. Remember that party back in the day?' He swigs more beer.

How can he bring that party up? As if I'd ever forget it.

'She dumped me that night. I'm pretty sure she's going to do the same to Ben when he turns up this evening. It's karma. I like that. Parallel lives. She won't be going anywhere.'

If only that were true, but I'm not taking what Gareth is telling me seriously. She wouldn't cheat on Ben. And if she did, she would tell me, I'm sure of it.

Just then, Ava and Steph come in from the garden. They stop in their tracks when Ava sees Gareth. He picks up the wine bottle with the rose in and hands it to her, his expression hopeful, making me feel sorry for him. She looks at him in horror and lets it drop. The bottle smashes on the white tiles, shards of green glass everywhere, petals scattering in a dark trail as the rose hits the floor.

'Ava, what's up?' Steph looks baffled, her eyes moving from Ava to the shattered bottle. 'You've gone completely white.'

'It's been you all along,' Ava says to Gareth, her voice quivering. 'All these years, you've been tormenting me, terrifying me.'

Steph grabs a broom from the corner of the room, her eyes crinkled with concern. 'What are you talking about?' she asks, sweeping the fragments of glass into a pile.

'The roses,' Ava says, her voice catching as if the words are scratching her throat. 'You've pretended to be my friend when all the time it's you who's been sending them to me.'

Gareth picks up the rose that is lying at his feet. 'I don't know what you're talking about. It was meant to be a nice gesture.'

'You could at least admit it. You're doing it because I don't want to be with you. You're just jealous of Ben.'

'Ben! He's not here. He can't even be bothered to come to your party.'

'He will be.' She throws me an anguished look, and I reach out, rub her arm.

'Long-distance relationships never work,' he says.

'When will you stop, Gareth? Why won't you listen? Surely you must have got the message by now? I'm leaving. I'm moving to New York. And after tonight, I never want to see you again.'

Gareth grips the back of the chair in front of him. 'You don't mean that.'

Steph puts the glass in the bin, looking concerned.

'Why haven't you told Lena about us?' he asks.

I pour myself a glass of rosé from a wine box on the table.

'Why haven't you told her?' Gareth asks again. 'Didn't that night mean anything to you? Let's hope Ben hurries up and gets here. Then we'll see what *he* thinks about what happened.'

Music thuds in the background and all eyes in the kitchen are on Ava. And not in a 'we're so happy to be here at your party and we're all wishing you a good send-off' way. She glances around, a panicked expression on her face, then rushes out of the room.

One pair of eyes in particular draws my gaze, deep-set and unblinking. What is *she* doing here? I blink, and she's no longer there.

CHAPTER 14

2005

Lena had to push Ava into the room, placing a discreet hand on her back. Danny was amongst a group of seven boys, and the only ones Ava knew were the older boys who were at school with Martha. This wasn't a good idea.

'Don't make me do this.' She was aware of the girls in the corner watching them, sniggering. It had been a mistake to come here, and she wished she were back in her bedroom, sitting on the floor and playing CDs.

Lena took her arm. 'They're just boys, Ava. If you had a brother, you'd know how insignificant they are. Well, mostly.' She threw a glance towards Danny, who was fooling around, laughing with his friend who was balancing a beer can on his forehead. 'I know exactly what you need.'

She dragged Ava into the kitchen, where the overhead light was on, making her blink at the unexpected brightness.

'Can I have a glass of water?' she asked. She sat on a wooden chair, glad that the kitchen was empty.

'Water?' Lena waved a hand to indicate the bottles and cans crammed onto the counter. 'What you need is a proper drink, settle your nerves.' She looked around at what was on offer, then peered into the punch bowl, pouring some into a plastic cup. 'More punch,' she said, 'strong, just like you need.'

'I'm not sure.' Ava didn't want to drink too much, but at least the cups were small.

Lena, however, ignored the stack of small glasses, taking a large one from the cupboard and filling it. The glass said *Guinness* on the side, which was what Lena's grandpa drank with his mates in the pub. He swore by it too – said the dark Irish stout was what kept him strong. Her grandma even had a can with her lunch.

Lena passed the glass of punch to Ava, who closed her eyes and took a mouthful. The liquid burned into her throat and stomach, making her cough. But she felt warmer, and after a few moments her whole body seemed to relax, followed by a little burst of adrenalin. Lena always knew what was best for her.

'Better?' Lena asked. 'You're not so deathly white now; your cheeks are pink.' She topped up the glass. 'Drink up.'

Ava was glowing now. She felt better, braver. Tingles all over her skin.

'Not too much,' she said. 'I don't want to be ill.'

'For goodness' sake, Ava. You're not turning into Martha, are you? Trust me, I've been drinking this stuff since I was thirteen. It's never done me any harm.'

'That's what I mean. Your body is used to it. Mine isn't.' Ava giggled. 'I think it's in shock right now.' She drank some more and laughed.

Someone turned the music up in the next room, and she jumped to her feet.

'I want to dance.' She started to jig about. 'I love this song.' It was a high-energy dance track with a bustling beat. Her heart raced along with the insistent thrum of the bass as if it might burst.

'That's better,' Lena said. 'Now, let's see if we can find you a cute boy to dance with.'

CHAPTER 15

Ava

'Ava. What just happened?' Lena is calling after me as I crash up the stairs. 'Have you had too much to drink?'

I rush past a woman who is waiting for the bathroom and go into my own room. I push against the door to close it, but Lena is right behind me, catching it in time as I fling myself face down on the bed. She sits down beside me and strokes my hair. Heat radiates from my body and I can feel sweat on my shoulders, making my scar itch like crazy. Footsteps crash up the stairs and someone yells. The bathroom door slams. Here in the bedroom, the music is muffled, and the room feels vast without all my possessions.

'I don't understand why you're so upset. Gareth is annoying, but ...' Her voice trails off.

I sit up. My mascara leaves black smudges on the stark white pillowcase, and I wipe the back of my hand across my cheek. What is the matter with me tonight? I never normally cry.

'Don't let him get to you. You know what he's like; everyone knows he puts you on a pedestal. Come on, we were joking about it with your dad earlier. Nobody will believe what he says. I'll have a word with him when I go down. He'll have to leave if he's going to upset you.'

'It's not about that. Well, it is, but ...'

'Take some deep breaths. There's a party downstairs, your party. You can't let him ruin the evening with his lies.'

She rubs her hand over my back and it instantly makes me feel better. I'm going to miss her so much. Tears well again and I sniff them away.

'Shh, shh, don't get yourself worked up. I'm here, remember, and you know I'll never let anyone hurt you, especially not him. Besides, everyone here is your friend.' She laughs, trying to lighten the mood, but a chill creeps down my spine at her words. 'Nobody even believes what he's saying.'

'That's not what this is about.'

'OK ...' Lena sounds confused.

She's quiet for a moment, the only sound in the room the vibration from the music downstairs.

'You can tell me anything, Ava.'

I take a deep breath.

'It's the rose that Gareth brought.'

'It wasn't the prettiest rose I've ever seen.' She shrugs. 'But it was a nice gesture.'

'You don't understand.'

'Try me.'

I pause. 'You know the rose that was left on the doorstep earlier? Well, another black rose was delivered to me this morning. Number thirteen.'

Lena frowns. 'Like the cake.'

'Exactly. I've been getting them ever since the accident. Always on the anniversary.' My voice is shaking as much as my hands. Saying it out loud makes it real, but it's a relief too. After all these years, I've finally told her. I clench my hands together.

'Ava, you shouldn't be counting them.'

'I don't believe you can't see the significance. Everything changed for you too.'

'Of course it did. But after the way I'd been dragged up, my life changed for the better. That's why I had to help make yours better too. If you're happy, then I'm happy. Twins, remember?'

'We need to speak to Gareth about it,' I say.

'But why would Gareth do this? It doesn't make sense.'

'Nothing Gareth does makes sense. He doesn't want to acknowledge I'm with Ben now, never has. Sending roses is bizarre, though, even for him.'

The first rose was a complete shock. It was a bad time already – the first anniversary. Even if I'd wanted to pretend it wasn't happening, I couldn't. School had arranged a special assembly, and the unveiling of a plaque and a water fountain dedicated to Tess. I refused to go in that day, but just to make sure I didn't forget, the rose arrived. A black rose, dark and ominous, sending shadows into my dreams.

On the second anniversary, as soon as I saw Mum holding the box, I knew. I told her it was a poster I'd ordered for a project and hurried upstairs to my room on trembling legs. I didn't want her to see how I was shaking all over at just the sight of it.

Going to university didn't stop the roses coming. When I received a card telling me to collect a parcel from the porters' lodge, it didn't even cross my mind that that was what it would be. But realising that whoever was sending them had tracked me there sent me into free fall. I didn't leave my room for a week, until Lena turned up, anxious because I hadn't been returning her messages, dragging me to the college nurse. Even then I didn't tell her about the roses; it was something I wanted to keep to myself, to try and pretend it wasn't happening.

Every anniversary after that, they arrived without fail. I've had nightmares for years in which I'm being smothered by huge dark petals, their softness fooling me into stroking them before I impale myself on a thorn. A sickly smell fills my nose and throat, and I can't breathe.

'So that's why you freaked out just now,' Lena says, dragging me away from my spiralling thoughts. 'I get it. I couldn't understand why you were letting Gareth bother you so much.'

She pauses. 'He implied something happened between you two. Is that true?'

'No.' The word shoots out of me like a firework. 'How could you think that? We kissed, that's all. It was a stupid mistake. I was totally out of it and I just wanted to get rid of him. But him turning up now with the rose changes everything.'

'It was that night he came back here, wasn't it?'

'Yeah, after the three of us had been out for a drink. You went to bed. I'd had a weird Skype call with Ben; he was in a funny mood, but when I asked him what was up, he denied anything was wrong. But you know when you just know? Gareth was on good form and managed to cheer me up. We had a brandy and it went straight to my head, and I let him kiss me. Of course I regretted it straight away.

'I woke up around four o'clock and went to get a glass of water, and he was asleep on the sofa. I was mortified. I made him leave immediately. It was a terrible mistake and he can't see it. He thinks it meant something, but turning up now with the rose … I don't want him to have some weird sort of hold on me. And I can't believe he's been sending them all these years.'

'What are you going to do about Ben? Does he know about Gareth?' Lena says, after a loaded silence.

'Of course not. There's nothing to know. It was only a kiss; it meant absolutely nothing to me, you must be able to see that. It was the stupidest thing I could have done. I've been beating myself up about it ever since. And he wouldn't have ever had to find out, but now … what am I going to do?'

'It's better off coming from you. You don't want him hearing it from Gareth, do you?' Lena stands up, heading towards the window. As she passes the wardrobe, her hands run across the row of empty coat hangers, rattling into the silence.

'Oh God, now I really need to know for sure whether Ben is coming. Maybe it would be better if he didn't. I have to find my phone.' I join her over by the window. Below us, a group of my work colleagues stand in a circle. Gareth is on his own further down the garden, puffing on a roll-up.

'It hurts, you know, that you can't confide in me,' Lena says quietly. 'First I found out that Martha's been in touch, and now this. Up until a couple of hours ago, I thought we told each other everything.'

'But I don't even tell Ben everything,' I say, guilt lacing my words. 'You know that. I never want him to find out about my past, who I really am. I hate having to be so secretive. It kills me.'

'I get that you can't tell Ben about that, of course I do, but why didn't you tell me about Gareth? That's different.'

'I was embarrassed, OK, and so ashamed. Every morning since, I've woken up feeling sick. I wish I could undo it. And now this nightmare. Gareth will tell Ben, of course he will. It's what he's always wanted. And I didn't tell you about the roses because I was frightened. Stupidly, I thought pretending it wasn't happening would make it go away. Like it wasn't real. I haven't told Ben about them either, obviously. Nobody knows about them.' I look down at Gareth, who is still outside. He's walking round in circles now, looking at the ground.

'You need to stay calm. Gareth is jealous, pure and simple. Ben knows what he's like; he also knows you do silly things when you're drunk. It's not that bad, trust me.'

'I don't know. Ben has very strong views on fidelity. This could blow us apart. Gareth's counting on it. And that's not all. I've never had a rose out of sequence before – they've always been on the day of the anniversary, like some sort of sick gift – and now there's been three in one day. And the cake. Is Gareth behind that too? How well do we really know him? We have no idea what he's capable of. I'm scared, Lena.'

CHAPTER 16

Lena

Ava finally moves away from the window. The way she's sitting on her bed, mascara streaked across her face, takes me back to the teenage Ava waiting for me to do her make-up for that first party. How different our lives might have been if we hadn't gone out that night. If she'd stayed home alone listening to her records and never got talking to Danny. I bet we'd have drifted apart years ago. My life would most certainly have been different. Imagine if David and Sue hadn't taken me in. With Dad going into rehab the summer of my GCSEs, I'd have had to go into care. My brother was in prison and there were no other relatives. The thought runs through me like ice-cold water. I can't believe she's been receiving these roses all this time. I can't believe she didn't tell me.

I'm shaking my head. 'For thirteen years. Did the roses come alone – I mean, was there a card or anything attached?'

'Always the same. A single rose in a box with a card with the number of the year on.'

'Have you kept them?'

She looks down at her hands. 'I couldn't bear to.'

'You should have done. For evidence. They could be dusted for fingerprints. The police can do wonders with forensics these days.' Ava's mouth wobbles as if she's going to cry again. 'Don't get upset. Now that I know, we can do something about it. I see why you wanted to pretend it wasn't happening, but you should have told me. We've always been able to rely on each other. You know I'll look after you.'

She nods. 'The one I received this morning gave me such a fright. I've had a doomed feeling this year; somehow the thirteenth anniversary seemed significant. I've wanted to tell you, almost did so many times, but I hoped it might go away. It's one of the reasons I finally made the decision to emigrate. To get away from all this.' She looks up at me. 'You must understand now why I have to go? It's such a relief to be able to explain properly at last. I'm sorry I didn't tell you, I hated keeping it from you. I know how devastated you are, and I am too, I love you, Lena, you're the best friend I've ever had, and nothing will get in the way of that no matter how many miles separate us. I'll never, ever forget what you did for me. If it wasn't for you, I wouldn't be here any more, and nobody can take that bond away from us. Not even Ben.'

'Oh Ava, that's such a lovely thing to say, and you know I feel exactly the same.' I pull her in for a hug. 'What are you going to do now that you suspect it's Gareth sending the roses?'

'I don't know. I didn't want to confront him in front of everyone; I just wanted to get out. I still can't see him being behind it, but I have to ask him. I'm not convinced jealousy would drive him to something like this. He's a link to the past, but not a serious proposition. You know what he's like; he's not clued up enough to organise something like that, year after year. I've even wondered about Martha.'

Just hearing the name makes me feel uncomfortable. I was right not to invite her this evening. Martha with her airs and graces, looking at me if as I'm something nasty under her shoe. 'What makes you think it could be her?'

'She's always resented you; she told me once that you were trying to take her place. I've tried to reach out to her a few times over the years, but she won't respond. She's holding on to a deep-seated grudge. On the other hand, given her glamorous lifestyle, she might not think about me at all. It's hard to know.'

'Much as I'd like to think it was her, you can't ignore the evidence in front of you. Gareth brought that rose into the house and we have to confront him. If he denies it, then we have to consider her as a possibility.'

'We can't do it in front of all my friends,' Ava says.

'We can be discreet. I don't want to scare you, but if he's sent two more roses today, maybe he's building up to something. And why roses? Do they have some kind of significance?'

'Believe me, I know all about roses. I've done my research. Red roses traditionally symbolise love, while white ones are often used at weddings to represent a new beginning, even peace. But a black rose isn't a natural thing; it's either bruised, decaying or it's been dyed to look darker. It symbolises death and loss, also anarchy. It's horrible. Somebody is trying to frighten me. And it's working, look.' She holds up her hands, which are trembling. 'When I saw Gareth with that rose, I was so scared.'

Biting her lip, she releases a strangled cry, and then she's sobbing, shoulders heaving, and I can't bear it. I sit on the bed and hold her tight. Her body shudders and she feels delicate in my arms. It's true, now I think about it; she hasn't been herself this year. I berate myself for not seeing it was more than work hassles. Now that it's all out in the open, maybe she won't need to run away.

'All night I've been excited that Ben might be coming, and now I don't want him here.' The shaking lessens and she gently pulls away from me. 'I can't have him involved in all this. Is he coming? Surely now you can let me know?'

It's the right time to tell her. I look at her and nod.

'Then why isn't he here yet? If it was the other way round, I'd be desperate to get to him. God, I wish I knew where my bloody phone was.'

'Even if you did find your phone, he won't be trying to get in touch with you because I asked him not to. I was worried he wouldn't be able to keep the party secret. He said he was excited, but …'

'But what?'

'I—'

The music downstairs stops and we both look at one another. For me it's a welcome distraction. I can't tell her now. Not when she's just pulled herself together. The music starts again, a different track this time.

'Come on, let's go down. Don't worry about Gareth. Tell you what, I'll ask him about it without giving anything away, OK?'

'Would you? That would really help. You're the best, Lena.'

We hug, and I grip my arms tightly around her, not wanting to let her go, ever; wanting to savour this special moment. Her hair feels damp. 'Try and stay away from him,' I say. 'And if it turns out to be Martha, we can deal with that later. After the party, which you are going to enjoy if it kills me. I've got your back, you know that.'

'I need to fix my face first,' she says, turning towards the bathroom.

'Do you want me to do it?'

'No, don't worry, it will give me a moment to compose myself. You go ahead.'

'Ava.' I stop her, taking a deep breath. 'I've been thinking … Maybe I could even come with you to America. There's nothing keeping me here, and I've always wanted to go to New York. I can take my business anywhere. It's always been me and you …' I pause, wait for her to say 'against the world', like we've done ever since we first met, but she remains silent. She might as well have hit me. 'You don't want me to come, do you?' The question sounds strangled.

She sighs. 'I told you how much you mean to me, but things are different now. I have to move on. I'm making my future with

Ben now. It'll be your turn soon; you'll find someone and you'll soon forget about me.'

I'm lost for words. I want to tell her how much I love her, how important she is to me, how I don't want to let her go. But instead I stay quiet, cheeks burning and heat rising in my body. My mind is racing. Maybe I should tell her about Ben, about *my* secret.

CHAPTER 17
2005

'Hey, Lena,' Danny said. Ava felt like a gooseberry, but she didn't want to leave Lena's side. She needn't have worried, though, as a boy appeared at her elbow, grinning widely.

'I'm Jon,' he shouted above the insistent bass of the music, which Ava couldn't help moving about to.

'Ava,' she said, moving away from Lena so that she could have Danny all to herself. She couldn't help notice Danny flicking a glance at her, taking in what she was wearing. She smoothed down her dress, the silky material soft under her sweating hands.

'You're Martha's sister,' Jon said, making her squirm inwardly. She hated being compared to her brainbox sibling. They were nothing like each other.

'Is she a friend of yours?' she asked.

'Not really.'

'We're very different,' she told him.

'That's good,' he said. 'We're not close at all, to be honest. She's a bit geeky for me.'

'Thank goodness for that.' Lena drank some more punch, still not used to the strong taste of the alcohol.

'Here.' Jon took her glass. 'Let me get us a couple of refills.'

Ava felt much more relaxed now she'd got someone to chat to. She smiled at him as he came back with two full glasses.

'It's very hot in here,' she said. 'Shall we go into the kitchen?'

Jon led the way through the room. He was easy to talk to and he made her giggle. They were both laughing when she heard her name being called. As she turned, she realised who it would be. Gareth. He was pushing through people to get to her, holding a single red rose. His face was flushed, as if he'd been running. She'd been having such a good time, she'd forgotten all about him. Now she felt a familiar lurch of worry. He was looking at Jon, and the muscles in his neck were straining as he tightened his jaw.

'I should have been here ages ago, but the bus broke down halfway and we had to wait ages for a replacement. I've been texting you,' he added. 'I wondered why you weren't answering. Here.' He held out the rose.

'Thanks.' It was wilting in the heat, the petals bruised.

'Have some punch,' Jon said. 'That will make you feel better. He sloshed some into a plastic glass. 'I'm Jon, by the way.'

Gareth glared at him. Ava wished he hadn't come. She'd been enjoying herself until then.

'I'm Gareth, and I'd like to dance with my girlfriend.'

Pathetic.

'I'm sorry,' Ava said to Jon. 'I'll be back; just something I need to sort out in private.' She hoped he could hear the words she wasn't saying: *Please don't let this idiot stop you from being friendly.*

She could feel Gareth's gaze drilling into her, giving her the momentum she needed to get it over with.

'I need to talk to you,' she said. 'Let's do this outside.'

As they headed to the back door, Gareth paused to grab a bottle of beer from the counter. Ava felt the prick of the rose thorn in her hand. She hurled the flower across the grass as soon as she stepped outside.

'Hey,' he said. 'I gave you that. It was meant to be special.'

Her mouth was so dry it was hard for her to speak, but she had to tell him. She thought of Lena, and how she wasn't afraid of anything. *Me and you against the world*, that was what they were always saying. Time to put it into practice; fake the bravery Lena showed. She lifted her chin and looked at his annoying collar, the way his hair hung over his eye, meaning she was never sure if he was looking at her or not.

'I want us to be friends,' she said.

'We are friends.'

'I mean *just* friends. I don't want to go out with you any more.'

Gareth's face crumpled, and she felt swamped with guilt.

'I'm sorry,' she said, cringing at the situation, then turned and ran back into the house to find Lena. Lena was right, she was always right. Ava didn't need anybody else.

CHAPTER 18

Ava

Lena leaves the room with a determined look on her face, and I'm transported back to her teenage bedroom, the tiny box room with clothes covering the once-pink threadbare carpet. Her dad was yelling at her, and even though it was nothing to do with me, my heart was thumping with fear. My parents never shouted at me like that. Lena slammed the door and kicked the bedpost. 'Asshole!' she yelled at the top of her voice. I tried to put my hand on her shoulder, but she shoved it off as if my palm was on fire. I didn't know how to calm her then and I am no wiser now.

My priority is getting hold of Ben, just as soon as I've patched up my face. Mascara-streaked eyes look back at me from the mirror, but I've only got essentials in my wash bag and wish I'd packed more stuff. Murky foundation mixes with tears and mascara on the cotton wool, removing the external signs of misery from my face. My hands tremble, in contrast to earlier, when Lena applied my make-up with her capable touch. My hair is still in place, but my face is drawn – smiling at the mirror doesn't work when my eyes are so anxious – and my high cheekbones make my face look sunken. Foundation and bronzer give me a bit of colour. Maybe it's time to tell Ben the truth, bring everything out into the open. But that won't make it go away. The thought leaves me feeling nauseous, and the bathroom lock takes ages to open with my fumbling fingers.

I put my case on its side and unzip it. Everything is neatly packed, and I slide my hand underneath my night clothes and feel for the envelope that contains my travel documents. Looking at my one-way ticket to JFK makes the adventure ahead real. Just the thought cheers me up. My finger traces over my name on the ticket, and I'm about to put it back when fear jolts me, making my hand recoil. Where's my passport? It should be in the envelope, but nothing slides out when I shake it.

I let out a cry. For once I'm desperate to see the terrible photo where my fringe is cut too short and I'm scowling at the camera, taken during my first days at university when looking after myself wasn't a priority until Lena turned up and took me in hand. Reaching under my clothes again, I feel around, but nothing has slipped out. I take everything out of the case and drop it on the floor, no longer mindful of my orderly packing. This can't be happening.

I'm on my knees, staring open-mouthed at the case, when the door opens and Steph sticks her head around it.

'There you are. You've been gone for ages. I came to see if you were all right. Oh love,' she says, when she sees the terror in my expression. 'It's all got too much for you, hasn't it? I've been waiting for you to crack. You've been like a coiled spring lately, so tense, what with Pete and everything. It was bound to happen; you have to let it out some time. Downstairs just now, with Gareth, what was all that about?'

I'm shaking my head at her words, which I can't think about now, dislodging my hair from the elegant updo I so carefully set it in earlier. 'My passport's gone.'

'Are you sure?'

I nod, picking up the envelope. 'It was in here, I was just looking at my ticket, reminding myself that I really am going. My passport was in here, I'm sure it was.'

'Let's think. When did you last see it?' She goes into the bathroom and gets me a glass of water. I sip it slowly and consider.

'I checked in on my phone. That's the last time I remember having it … Yes, I packed it when I was at Mum and Dad's.' My head is aching with everything that has been happening, hundreds of thoughts hammering at my brain, and I'm unable to recreate the scene in my mind. 'I was in the kitchen, Mum was talking to me. I guess I was distracted. I could ring her.'

'It's bound to be there.'

'I hope I'm doing the right thing,' I say.

'What do you mean?'

'Going to live with Ben.' The scar on my shoulder is burning, and I rub at it with my fingers. 'It's hard being apart. I can't help wondering what he gets up to out there.'

'Ava! He wouldn't have asked you to move over there if he wasn't sure. And why would he want anyone else? Look at you, you're beautiful.'

I give a rueful smile. 'Sometimes lately my mind works overtime.' The kiss with Gareth flashes into my mind. If it can happen to me, what's to say Ben wouldn't do the same? 'But I'm sure you're right, and once we're living together, I'll realise I've been imagining things.'

'Of course you will. And if it doesn't work out—' She sees my stricken expression. 'Don't look at me like that. Nothing in life is certain, but whatever happens, we'll all be here for you.'

A burst of loud laughter interrupts us. Steph takes my hand and pulls me up.

'Let's go down and join in, see what's so funny. It's your party, Ava; all these people are here for you. Ignore those few idiots that you don't want to see – you'll never have to speak to them again after tonight. It's a really good party. Lena has put a lot of work into organising it. Loads of people are dancing, badly. It's worth seeing – might even cheer you up.' She moves a strand of hair from my cheek. 'Come on, let's get drunk together; it's the last chance we'll have for ages.'

'But what if I can't find my passport? I can't bear to even think about that.'

'And you mustn't. Promise me. Tomorrow you can worry about it all you like, though you won't need to because it's bound to be at your parents'. Tonight is hedonistic decadence from now on. OK?' She grips my shoulders and looks at me with determined eyes.

She's right. I'll forget about the passport for tonight, as well as my missing phone. And since I've no way of getting hold of Ben, I'll just have to be patient and wait for him to get in touch. He will, I know he will. I rub my finger, imagining my ring shining there, and feel better just thinking about my precious secret.

'You're on. Let's go and get a drink.'

I check my face briefly in the mirror before following her down the stairs. Esther, my friend from the gym, emerges from the lounge.

'Ava, there you are. Everyone's been wondering where you'd got to.' She gives me a hug. 'Lovely party, thanks so much for inviting me. Lucky you, eh, gorgeous fellow, the Big Apple. Want to swap lives by any chance?'

The doorbell goes. 'I'll get it,' says Steph. 'Be with you in a sec.'

I'm relieved to see that neither Lena nor Gareth is in the kitchen.

Esther peers into the punch bowl. 'We're running low – can't have that.'

She looks around the kitchen, spots a bottle of rum on the side and pours in a generous slug, topping it up with orange juice and lemonade.

'Here you go,' she says. She hands me a glass and touches hers against mine, rather too forcefully, as the liquid sloshes over the rim of the cup, leaving a red drop on my hand. I rub it away. 'To you and your big adventure.'

The punch leaves a fiery taste at the back of my mouth, making me cough.

'Whoops, have I overdone it?'

I can't stop coughing, and I indicate to Esther that I'm going outside. In the garden, I breathe in deep lungfuls of air, welcoming a moment to myself. The bonfire is still going and one of Felix's friends is standing beside it. I fancy talking to someone completely new who knows nothing about me, who doesn't see the layers that cover me like a shroud, and I'm about to go over when a figure emerges in front of me. It's Pete.

'Don't look so alarmed,' he says, but he's blocking my path and nobody else is around. An image flashes before me – me backed up against the wall, him close enough for me to see the silver flecks in his beard – and my throat tightens. *Just like last time.*

Over his shoulder there is movement in the kitchen, and I hold my breath, hoping that more people will come outside, but whoever is in there moves over to the table; they'll be making choices about what they fancy to eat, and I wish I had the choice not to be here with this man who I loathe and who has no right to be here. I feel a flash of anger at both Lena and Steph for letting this happen. Steph should have made sure Pete knew he wasn't welcome tonight. But I know I'm being unfair. She's been the one making me coffee and providing a sympathetic ear during my many shaky moments at work, when I've caught Pete looking at me from behind his office window, always watching.

'Can we talk?' He lights a cigarette and I take a discreet step backwards.

I notice there are three people over by the tree, and the girls from the office are talking to Kate by the back door. Why can't Pete be interested in any of them?

'You didn't bring your girlfriend?' I ask, a redundant question, but I want to remind him he's spoken for.

'We split up months ago. I don't see your fiancé either.'

'He's not here yet,' I say, finishing my drink so I can get away from this hulking man in his too-tight shirt, whose aftershave reeks even out here in the garden with the bonfire blazing. The three-some under the tree are going into the house, and my pulse rises.

'I'm getting another drink,' I say, trying to sound strong. Lena would have no problem telling Pete where to go. I glance at the kitchen door, which looks so inviting, willing her to appear, but the same group of girls are there, Kate throwing her head back with laughter. She looks good fun and I wonder why she's never been out to the pub with us. I avoid looking at Pete and take a step towards the house, but he puts his hand on my arm to stop me. I shake it off.

'Leave me alone.'

'Please, Ava,' he says, pulling his hand back. 'I just wanted to apologise for that little misunderstanding we had. You don't have to leave; it's a total overreaction. You're an asset to the company. We can discuss your role, look at your salary, see what other perks are available.'

Watching him standing there pleading with me, I see him for what he is. An insecure middle-aged man unable to admit what he's done. The alcohol I've consumed fuels my bravado. I won't let him spoil anything else in my life. Especially not my party.

'You did me a favour, actually,' I say. 'You helped me make up my mind.'

'Ava.' Steph emerges from the back door and walks across the lawn. 'I wondered where you were. More people have just arrived; a couple of friends from your old music club, I think.'

I flash her a smile to convey that I'm grateful, and move towards her.

'You OK?' she asks as we walk back to the house. 'I freaked out when I saw you stuck out there with him. How did that happen?'

'I stepped outside for some fresh air, didn't see him lurking. He tried to persuade me to stay at the charity. Unbelievable.'

'No way. He's such a creep. I hate him for driving you away. Why doesn't he ever go anywhere with his girlfriend?'

'They're over, so he says.'

'He shouldn't be here. I'm sorry about the mix-up with the invite. I've spoken to Lena and we both feel terrible about it.'

'Forget it, it's done now.'

'Exactly. Two days and you'll be out of here.'

The drone of an aeroplane overhead makes us both look up. I see the faraway dot of light in the sky and my heart thuds. What if I can't find my passport? Without it, I won't be going anywhere.

CHAPTER 19

Lena

Gareth is standing by the bonfire, staring into the flames.

'Ava's really upset,' I say, my voice low. 'Why did you bring the rose? Wasn't leaving one on the doorstep earlier enough? What exactly are you trying to achieve?'

His thick eyebrows knit together as he scratches his thatch of hair. 'I've no idea what you're talking about. I brought one rose. It was meant to be a nice gesture. Ladies like flowers, don't they?'

'It wasn't exactly beautiful. It had seen better days, you've got to admit.'

He drinks from the bottle of beer he's holding. 'If I'd brought a bouquet, it would have been over the top. I can't win, can I?' He sighs. 'If I'm honest, it was on the wall outside; I picked it up on the spur of the moment. Wish I hadn't now. I didn't realise it would turn out to be such a big deal.'

'You found it outside. Are you sure?'

'Yes, of course.'

'Did you see who left it there?'

He shakes his head.

'So you haven't sent her black roses before?'

The bemused look he throws me convinces me he's telling the truth.

'You really think I'm a weirdo, don't you?' he says.

We both laugh, and the tension between us dissipates.

'Ava told me what happened,' I say, holding my hands out towards the fire to warm them. I keep my voice soft; I don't want to alienate him. 'She knows it shouldn't have happened. You've got to understand that she's with Ben now. She's flying across the world to be with him.' The words catch in my throat, the sentence strangled into a hiss.

'Why did she kiss me, then?'

'She'd had too much to drink, you know how it is.'

His cheeks burn and I can't help feeling sorry for him. 'Why does she even bother staying in touch with me?'

'Because she likes you as a friend, but if you keep pushing it, you will lose her. She's really upset. Is that what you want?'

'Of course not. Look, I won't say anything to Ben. That was bravado talking in there. I hate seeing her upset, just like you do. We're not so different, you and me.'

'Oh yeah, how do you make that out?'

'We both love her and don't want her to go. Don't pretend you're not gutted too.'

The wind gets up and the flames flicker wildly, spitting in my direction. I experience a rush of emotion as I contemplate everything and realise what is happening. The roses are driving Ava away; she is running from a past she can never escape. Gareth and I are both part of that past. Tomorrow Ava will be gone and she won't have me to protect her any longer, to cover her secrets. I don't want this night ever to end.

I'm not in the mood for conversation when I wander back into the kitchen. The punch is darker in colour than it was, a murky brown now, and an empty rum bottle stands beside it. I grab a mug from the side and fill it. The potency hits me as I take a swig, and my head swirls. I drink some more. Laughter spills in from the garden, while I'm stuck in here feeling like a fool. Ava *wants* to get away from me. Her words cut into me like knives.

Two women are standing in the doorway talking. The one with the sharp black bob turns and steps into the kitchen, her dark painted eyes fixed on me. My heart thuds against my chest.

'What are you doing here?' I ask in a whisper.

'Chill, Lena. I couldn't resist it. It's a decent party.' She helps herself to a cracker topped with a swirl of cheese and celery and bites into it. The crunching noise grates on my nerves.

'You shouldn't be here. Ava doesn't know you and I want it to stay that way. This is her party.'

'So what? You organised everything; why can't you have some of your own friends here?'

'You're not my friend.'

'Doesn't matter. She works with my partner. Pete also invited me.'

'You know Pete? How?' The coincidence makes my head spin. Kate and Pete? It doesn't make sense.

She picks up another cracker. 'Sure I do. Me and Pete go way back. Had a bit of a fling once upon a time. Can't remember what I saw in him now, though.'

She's interrupted by the sound of the doorbell, and I breathe a sigh of relief and hurry out into the hall.

Someone has left a glass of wine on the windowsill to the side of the front door. The wood of the door sticks and I pull hard. A woman is standing on the step with her back to me. Dyed red shoulder-length hair, expensive leather jacket and tailored jeans, standing tall in her high-heeled boots. Smart, vaguely familiar. She turns, and I see the flawless face I was looking at only last week in a magazine. Ava's sister, Martha.

'Lena. I might have guessed you'd be here.' Her eyes flick up and down my body. 'My invitation appears to have got lost in the post. I bet Ava didn't tell you she invited me to stop by.'

I'm still staring in shock, unable to form any words.

'Thought not. I could hear the music as soon as I got out of my car.' She glances at the expensive-looking Fiat parked outside the house. 'Sounds like a good party. Aren't you going to ask me in?'

'You weren't invited for a reason,' I say. Ava can't have invited her; she would have said so earlier. Wouldn't she?

'I'm Ava's sister, Lena, her *blood* sister, and it's time we sorted things out. That's why I'm here. I care about Ava, always have done. You don't want to stop me coming in, do you? I wouldn't recommend it. I can make quite a fuss.' She puts the pointed toe of her boot on the doorstep, forcing me to step back.

At that precise moment, my phone beeps with a text. I make a point of pulling it out of my pocket in front of her, my body blocking hers. When Ben's name flashes up on the screen, I wish I hadn't. Martha arches an eyebrow at me.

'Interesting,' she says. 'What's my sister's boyfriend texting you for? I assumed he'd be here.'

'Not yet. It's part of the surprise.' Why am I even telling her? It's none of her business. I shove the phone back into my pocket and move aside to let her in. A blast of cold air wafts into the house at the same time.

'At least she'll be getting away from you,' she says.

Her words land like heavy raindrops. Ava doesn't want to leave me, she doesn't.

'Martha.' Ava has come out of the kitchen. She looks stunned to see her sister. It's clear she doesn't know whether to embrace her or not, as if unsure of the protocol after the past few frosty years. My hands itch to snatch her away, but it's too late. Martha takes the initiative and holds out her arms.

'Come here, you. I'm so happy to see my baby sister.'

That last comment is for my benefit. Insincere. *Don't fall for it, Ava.*

Martha fixes her eyes on mine as she squeezes Ava to her. Ava's words are running through my head: *She's always resented you; she told me once you were trying to take her place.*

My chest tightens as I hold her gaze.

I won't let you take my place either.

CHAPTER 20

2005

Ava ran into the house, forcing herself to slow down as she looked for Lena.

'Your mate's gone to the bathroom,' a girl said.

Ava risked a quick look behind her, but Gareth hadn't followed her in. Her chest puffed in and out and she helped herself to another glass of punch from the bowl on the table, willing her heart to calm down. The feeling of absolute mortification evaporated and was replaced by a burst of euphoria. She'd done it. Her body felt weightless as the alcohol slid into her bloodstream and the music swelled in her head. She was itching to get onto the dance floor as soon as Lena came back, and she had a little boogie by herself while she topped up her glass again.

A girl came towards her holding an empty plastic cup, and Ava laughed aloud, not feeling nervous or self-conscious for once. Why shouldn't she be dancing around the kitchen? She was a single girl and could do whatever she wanted. Lena had been urging her to lighten up for long enough, and tonight she was going to take her advice.

The girl frowned, and Ava stopped dancing. Oh no. It was Tess, Martha's best friend. Her stomach convulsed.

'Hello, Ava, what are you doing here?'

Ava held herself very still, Tess wasn't as studious and boring as Martha, but Ava didn't want her to know she'd been drinking.

If Tess told Martha she'd been at this party, this party at an older boy's house, she'd be in all sorts of trouble. Grounded for weeks. *Lying is wrong, Ava.* But Lena called it twisting the truth. Lena helped Ava to be fun, to be a better version of herself.

'Ava?' Tess said. She had such a friendly face, and she'd always been nice to Ava. But that didn't mean she wouldn't get her into trouble.

'I'm with Lena, it's her friend Danny's party. She didn't want to come on her own.'

'Does Martha know you're here?'

'Martha's away.'

'I know she is. That's not what I asked. Does she know?'

'Probably not. We don't get on that well, you must know that.' *Please don't mention Mum and Dad.*

'Do your parents know?'

In the next room, the music track changed, sounding even louder. Ava's feet itched to go and dance.

'They don't. Please don't tell them. They don't like Lena. Going to a party with anyone else wouldn't be a problem, they wouldn't mind that.'

It was true. Her parents weren't overly strict as long as she was sensible. But when it came to Lena, it was a whole other story.

She had an idea. 'Let me get you a glass of punch. It's really nice. Sweet, fruity.' She reached for the ladle and missed. 'Whoops.'

Tess shook her head, smiling. 'I can see you've had some already. Don't overdo it, Ava, will you? I can't drink anyway, I'm driving.' She grinned and jangled a bunch of keys. 'I passed my test. First time. Dad bought me an old Mini and it's parked outside. No way am I going to drink and drive, not one drop. I've been waiting years for this.'

'That's so cool.'

'Are you still going out with Gareth?' Tess asked.

Ava shook her head. 'He's not right for me. I've just told him, actually. Was that terrible, telling him here? Look.' She showed Tess the string of recent texts on her phone. 'That's just this evening.'

Tess shook her head. 'If it doesn't feel right … Not that I'm an expert, but I'd say you've done the right thing.'

'That's what Lena said.'

'There you go then. Great minds as they say.'

Ava smiled. Lena was right, she was always right. 'I wish you'd tell Martha that. She can't stand Lena. But thanks. Please don't drop me in it, Tess.'

Tess twisted her car keys round, looping them on and off her finger, as if they might give her some answers. She liked to do the right thing and be responsible, but Ava was a good kid and there was a chilled-out atmosphere at the party, with teenagers chatting and laughing good-naturedly. Maybe they were drinking a little too much, but it was no drug-fuelled rave. And she liked Lena; the girl had a tough home life and deserved a break from Martha, who was too judgemental.

'Don't worry. I won't mention seeing you. I promised Danny I'd drop by, but I'm not staying long. Just go easy on the punch, and keep yourself safe.'

Lena appeared in the doorway, wiping her hands on her thighs.

'Come and dance,' she said, before she spotted Tess. Her eyes rounded at Ava. 'Oh.'

Tess smiled. 'You girls go.'

Lena danced into the living room and Ava followed her, feeling a buzz of relief, then a burst of energy. This was going to be the best night ever.

CHAPTER 21

Ava

Martha smells of expensive perfume, and the soft leather of her jacket is cool against my skin. As she folds her arms around me, the buttery smell of her skin jolts my memory and the last few years fall away. Unexpected tears spring into my eyes.

'What are you doing here?' I say, stepping back and looking at her. The rounded cheeks of her teenage years have settled into a heart shape, and not a line creases her forehead. Must be Botox; she's the kind of woman who hates ageing, and she's got the money to do whatever she needs to keep the lines from her immaculately made-up face.

'Mum rang me, said I should get my arse down here before you leave the country. New York – get you. It's a fabulous place; that city has a vibe like no other. And it's about time, too – you and Ben have been an item forever. Don't look so surprised. Mum's always kept me updated on what you're up to.' She leans in and whispers in my ear. 'I told the lovely Lena a little white lie, that you'd invited me. I couldn't resist – she's so easy to wind up.'

'Martha!' I glance at Lena, who sighs loudly. Martha laughs, and I'm transported back to my childhood bedroom, my sister entering without knocking in that infuriating way she had, interrupting my homework to warn me against the 'undesirable friend' I'd been hanging round with at school. The rows that ensued. The air of frostiness that evaporated when Martha packed her bags and left hovers for a moment, and I'm a teenager again, caught between the two of them.

'Come into the kitchen,' I say. 'Let me get you a drink.'

Martha produces a bottle of champagne from her bag. 'I brought you this by way of apology, if you'll accept it.'

'Thank you.' The gesture thaws the atmosphere a little, but the cold touch of the bottle reminds me that we still have lots to sort out.

Esther and some of the other guests have congregated around the table, filling the air with loud voices. I wonder if anyone will recognise my sister. Outside, I can see people moving around near the shed, sorting out the fireworks, no doubt. The small garden table is empty.

'Let's sit in the garden,' Martha says. 'It'll be easier to talk out there.' She's taking charge, just like she always did.

I glance behind me to see whether Lena has followed us, but there's no sign of her.

'I'll just get some glasses,' I say. Unable to see any clean ones, I wash a couple in the sink. Perhaps Lena was right about the plastic glasses being naff – especially having to re-use them. I wonder if my parents knew when they were here earlier that Martha was planning on coming.

'I see you've still got your piano,' she says. 'Mum said you were playing again. I'm glad for you.'

I'm just about to step outside when Dave from work appears.

'Ava, there's a woman who's been taken ill upstairs. I thought you'd want to know. Sorry to bother you.'

'Anyone would think this was a teenage party,' Martha says, and I see a flash of my old condescending sister, followed by an image of me hurtling inside from a garden. A reminder of teenage parties I do not need. 'I'll come up with you. Our celebration will have to wait.'

Celebration is not the word I would have used; typical Martha getting ahead of herself. Lena certainly won't be celebrating, judging by the look on her face when Martha arrived. I want Lena to be OK after everything she's done for me this evening; for her to laugh and dance and enjoy the party with me. For her to give me her blessing. The importance of this tugs at my heart. Martha's only been here two minutes, and I'm caught between the two of them. New York can't come fast enough.

I keep my head down as I walk back through the kitchen, not wanting to be drawn into conversation with the group round the table. When I get to the top of the stairs, I see Lena in the bathroom doorway with Kate, and another woman kneeling on the floor, groaning.

'Is she OK?' Martha asks.

Kate has a strange look on her face. She frowns at Martha, then glances away quickly, avoiding her gaze. She's recognised her, that's what that look is. The crinkling of the forehead, the quizzical eyes. It must happen all the time. Martha completely ignores her, smoothing her hair back with her manicured nails.

'Give her some space,' she says. 'She doesn't need loads of people crowding her.'

'You chose to follow Ava up here,' Lena says, without making eye contact. 'How are you feeling, Sharon?'

'I want to go home,' the woman says. I didn't recognise her without her Lycra vest and leggings, hair tied up in a high ponytail. Zumba class on Tuesdays. Sharon is one of the handful of women I invited from the gym, in a fit of enthusiasm after they'd admired my engagement ring over a post-exercise smoothie. I couldn't resist showing them the velvet box, with the ring nestling inside, swearing them to secrecy. Now I run my fingers over the smooth skin of my naked ring finger, the delicious knowledge making me tingle all over, followed by guilt at keeping it from Lena.

'Is your coat in the bedroom?' Kate asks.

Sharon nods. 'It's a leopard-print jacket.' She splashes water on her face and groans. 'Sorry, I'm so sorry, this is so embarrassing.

But that punch – what on earth did you put in it? I only had two glasses and it made me throw up.'

'I think someone added a whole bottle of rum to it,' Lena says.

'Classy,' Martha says, and Lena visibly bristles.

'God, no wonder it made me sick.' Sharon pushes straggly hair out of her face and takes her coat from Kate, who leads her off down the stairs, holding her arm as if she might break. 'I've called you a cab,' she tells her. Martha stays in the doorway, her nose wrinkled at the smell. Lena crouches down and wipes the floor with a cloth.

'Let me help you,' I say.

'I've got it sorted.' Lena doesn't look up. Her shoulders are taut, her muscles straining. A plaster peeps out from under the strap of her dress; her tattoo. She swipes at the tiles with jerky movements, knocking against the side of the bath.

'Does this remind you of anything?' she asks.

'What do you mean?'

'You leaning over the toilet spewing your guts, me holding you steady, wiping sick from your hair. It used to happen a lot when we were teenagers. Your mum looked down on me then; she didn't realise how much time I spent looking after you.'

'I wasn't used to drinking.' We both laugh at the shared memory. 'And you know Mum hasn't seen you in that way for years.'

She sighs. 'But now that you're leaving, everything is going to be so different.'

'Change happens, deal with it,' Martha says, and Lena glares at her.

'Don't be like that, Lena,' I say. 'My parents will never stop loving you, and neither will I. But this is happening. You can't just ignore it and hope it will go away. You need to live your own life now.'

'Let me come with you,' she says.

Martha hoots with laughter.

'Maybe you could wait outside?' I suggest to my sister, not wanting to be stuck between the two of them in this enclosed space.

'I'll be on the landing,' she replies, leaving the room and shutting the door.

'It wouldn't work,' I say quietly to Lena. I can't help feeling sorry for her. I stand up, catching sight of my face in the mirror. My hair has gone limp, and I fluff it up, pinch a little colour into my cheeks. I look like I need a good long sleep. 'You've got your job here, your friends. You can't just leave your life behind.'

'But as a make-up artist I can work anywhere. And anyway, none of that means anything to me if you're not here. We need each other, Ava. I worry you won't cope on your own.'

'Won't cope? How old do you think I am? Besides, I'm with Ben now.'

Her cheeks flame. 'I don't trust him. He doesn't know you like I do. We go back years; think of how much history we have, everything we've been through. You're my family, Ava, you're like a sister to me.'

I can't believe what she's saying. 'Why don't you trust Ben? You hardly know him.'

'Have you ever wondered why it has to be you who moves to New York? Why can't he come back to London? He puts himself first, always has done. I just want you to be sure. I'm not convinced he's committed to you.'

'That's where you're wrong.' Again I touch my empty finger. 'The thing is …' my throat seizes up, but I force myself to say it, 'we're getting married. We've set the date and everything. I want to spend the rest of my life with Ben, and nothing you do or say will change that.'

The words are out and it's too late to take them back. Ben and I agreed we wouldn't tell Lena until I was in America. He's been saying for ages that she's too clingy. Instead of seeing her constant presence in Cambridge as supportive, he saw it as odd, couldn't understand why she didn't want to make her own life and her own friends. Of course he would see it like that; he doesn't know how much I need her, how beholden to her I am. What she did for me. Which is, ironically, why I need to get away from her. But it's so hard.

She gazes at me, lost for words.

'Married? And you didn't tell me?'

'Ben wanted us to announce it together. It makes sense now; he must have meant at the party, although I don't get why he isn't here yet.' A niggle of doubt wriggles up like a worm from the soil.

'You'll be getting married over here, right?'

'No, we'd like to get married in New York.'

'Why get married over there? You hardly know anyone in America; all your friends and family are over here.' Her lips plump into a pout and I try to ignore the sting of her words. Wrenching myself away from Lena was always going to be a challenge. After everything we've been through, when she literally saved my life, it was never going to be easy leaving her behind. Ben and I spent hours talking it over, planning. He was dismissive of Lena's feelings; he said she needed to grow up and stop being so childish. The protective feeling I got when he said that sweeps over me now, my fists curling automatically in her defence. *Only one more day to get through.*

'It's not going to be that kind of wedding. We're keeping it small. Just the two of us and witnesses.'

'You could have done that here.'

'This way is more beneficial.'

'In what way?'

I should never have started this conversation.

'Beneficial for who?' She's persistent, fixing me with a steely glare.

'For me. It gives me more rights.'

'Rights? You mean …' Lena's face drops as realisation dawns on her. 'You're not planning on coming back, are you?'

'No. I don't know. This way gives us options. You know what the United States is like. It's really complicated – so much red tape to get through – and Ben is looking into the possibilities. Nothing has been decided, Lena, honestly. It's bound to take ages. Think about the positives. Who wouldn't want a best friend in New York? You'll always have free accommodation. Steph is already arranging a Christmas shopping trip. You know you'll be welcome any time.' Ben will come around, I'm sure.

Lena remains crouched on the floor, an anguished look on her face. She drops her head into her hands.

'Leave me alone,' she says.

'Lena, please …'

'Just go.'

CHAPTER 22

Lena

I'm crouched on the floor, wiping up sick. Ava has told me she's getting married, and my world is spinning with all these changes. And Martha is prowling around on the landing, keeping tabs on my every move. Ava moves towards the door.

'No, wait,' I say. 'I want you to explain this to me. Were you even going to invite me? Would I just have got a text saying *oh, by the way …*? I can't believe you'd hide this from me.'

She looks at me guiltily.

'And I'm worried. I'm worried that you're making a huge mistake. How well do you really know him?'

She sits down on the side of the bath, twirling her hair round and round, pulling it tight.

'You know exactly how well I know him. Why are you doing this? Why are you saying these things all of a sudden?'

A sigh escapes me. During the party isn't the best time to bring it up, but I can't hold back any longer. Not after this revelation.

'Because I'm concerned for you, OK? He should be here by now. He arrived in London hours ago, said he'd be here early, and I'm not sure where he is.'

'What?' Ava stands up, her face creased with concern. 'Why didn't you say something earlier? Give me your phone, let me ring him.'

'Sure, as long as you know his number.'

'Not by heart, but you have it, don't you?'

'Why would I have it?'

'To organise the party, of course.'

'You've never given it to me. I've been emailing him. I'm surprised you don't know the number. Especially as he's your *fiancé*.'

'Oh you're impossible.' But she's rattled now, I can see it, roaming around the small space, rubbing her arms as if she's cold. The smell of vomit lingers in the air. The door opens and a whoosh of air sweeps through, blowing the smell into my face. I stand up, needing to get out. Martha sticks her head around the door. She must have been waiting outside.

'Are you two OK in here?' she asks, and Ava pulls a face. I barge past them, not wanting to witness this sisterly reconciliation, slamming the door behind me.

The thud of the music fills the house, adding to my hyped-up mood. Seeing Martha was bad enough, but the news of the engagement sticks in my throat. How could Ava had hidden it from me? My chest is heaving as if I've run a marathon and my throat is tight. Is this what a panic attack feels like?

I kick the door of my room shut behind me and survey the mess. Coats have been thrown in a heap on the bed and some have slid onto the floor. The dressing table is covered with my make-up from earlier and my rumpled clothes are strewn over the floor. The wardrobe is crammed, and I've got at least twenty boxes of shoes, mostly my trainer collection. My hair and beauty products fill three shelves. All of it has to be packed away and moved out tomorrow. And I don't really want to stay with Stacey. David's words from earlier come back to me, telling me it was for my own good. Did Ava know about it too, did she agree? The thought stabs at my soul. Everything Ava has told me tonight makes me think I can no longer trust her, if I ever could. Her getting married is the last straw. She's not even wearing an engagement ring. Is that because she's been hiding that from me too?

Something shifts inside me and I lose it completely, sweeping my arm across the dressing table and knocking everything to the floor. A mug of half-drunk cold tea bounces off the wall and I scream at my surroundings, kicking at the piles of clothes on the floor. My voice is swamped by the party sounds that rumble under the floorboards. I hate, hate, hate my life and I hate her for doing this to me. I catch sight of my contorted face in the mirror, my mouth pulled into a snarl, and I can't help comparing it with Martha's twisted sneer. I hurl the mirror to the floor, where it smashes to pieces. Seven years' bad luck – what do I care?

Someone knocks on the door. I ignore it. Another knock, louder.

'Go away,' I say. The door opens and Martha appears. I go to close it in her face, but she leans against it.

'Leave me alone.'

'For God's sake, Lena.' She pushes forward into the room until we're facing one another, my chest heaving in and out. 'Are you all right?' she asks.

'What do you care?'

'Let's try and be adult about this. We should talk. I care about my sister.'

'Not for the last … how many years is it? About twelve. I'm the one who cares about Ava, who's been there for her no matter what. You just left her to it.'

'Because I couldn't stand to stick around and watch the way you wheedled your way into our family, conning my parents, making yourself out to be such a hero. Look at you now, showing your true self, throwing a tantrum and trashing your room. I'm thrilled Ava is cutting herself off from you.'

Her words send a chill through my body. 'Cutting herself off' sounds so final, like a head under the guillotine. A sense of dread is creeping into my mind. Would she really abandon me like this?

Martha stands there looking poised and glamorous in the chaos of clothes and shattered glass. She looks around at the mess, then stoops to pick up a framed article that I've knocked from the wall.

'I don't believe it,' she says. 'You've had this on your wall all these years. I bet you look at it and congratulate yourself every day. You just can't let it go, can you?'

We both look at the newspaper cutting she's holding, the paper yellowing with age, the glass cracked, only the metal frame still in one piece.

'"Teenage hero",' she reads, in her precise, clipped voice. Rage swirls. How dare she mock me?

'You're just jealous because you weren't there for her and you hated your sister preferring me,' I say.

'Listen to yourself. I left that stuff behind years ago. You're still a disturbed teenager, stuck in the past. You haven't featured in my mental space for years.'

'Get out,' I tell her. 'I don't want you and your lies in my room.'

'But it's not your room for much longer, is it, Lena, and then where will you go? Don't even think about coming begging to my parents. Have you been wondering why they aren't opening their arms to you for a second time, welcoming you in? I've made them see sense; that it's time for you to make your own way in the world.'

'Get out.' I step towards her, my arm twitching like it does when I'm at my Boxfit class, Martha taking the place of the red leather punchbag in front of me. I clamp my hands together to stop myself from lashing out. I know too well the consequences of acting on my instincts and thinking later.

'You need help. Now stay away from my sister.'

She slams the door and I focus on the grooves in the wood as it rattles in the frame. Voices from outside draw me to the window. Out in the back garden a small group of people are crowding around. A man shifts, and I see orange flames flickering. I realise

I no longer care about the smooth running of the party. I shrug, even though there's nobody to witness my indifference.

But I do care about this house. I care deeply. From the first sighting of it, I knew it was the perfect house for Ava, the house to entice her away from her parents, who made it too easy for her. Easy for me too, undoubtedly, though the threat of Martha was never far away. She didn't stop visiting when I was there; just made it clear I wasn't welcome. Sue would encourage me out of the house, cheeks pink, words falling too fast out of her mouth, apologetic about her elder daughter and knowing I wouldn't – couldn't – make a fuss. This house got me away from that threat; it was Martha-free. As I stand here with my possessions in disarray around me, anger rises in me like the smoke that coils up from the bonfire, the smell creeping through the open window and filling the room. Martha has invaded this space too.

Loud voices rise from the garden and I watch as Steph hands out sparklers, looking towards the house, calling for Ava, who emerges from the kitchen, unsteady on her heels. The slingback stilettos were another present from Ben, a surprise in the post. She knows I don't have the money for such grand gestures, but I'm here for her and that's what she needs. Steph hands her a sparkler and they all write words and patterns onto the black of the night sky. In their midst, the fire is burning steadily, consuming the hours we have left this evening, yellow sparking like the flash from a camera.

A figure catches my eye. Martha is standing in a corner of the garden, smoking a cigarette. Steph passes a sparkler to a girl who has just joined the group. Dark hair, leather trousers; Kate. She shouldn't be here. She moves closer to Ava as they chat and nod, Kate laughing at something, throwing her head back, moonlight picking out the sheen of her jet-black hair. Then she glances upwards and catches sight of me in the window.

She says something to the person next to her and moves away from the fire. Holding her sparkler high, she starts to writes a word in the air, her movements slow and precise. I know straight away what it is going to be. The whole time, Martha looks on, eyes flicking between Kate and me as if watching the ball fly across the net at a tennis match.

I blink, and Martha is gone, her presence replaced by a cold dread in the pit of my stomach. Does she know?

CHAPTER 23

2005

'What were you talking to her for?' Lena asked Ava. 'She's one of your sister's stuck-up friends.'

'She's not stuck-up, she's really nice.'

'Aren't you worried she'll go running to Martha?'

'No, she won't.'

'That's what you think.' Lena had been brought up not to trust anyone outside of her family, and those inside it – well they were even worse.

'Don't, Lena.'

'Don't what?'

'Push everyone away. Tess is really friendly. I've just had a nice conversation with her; she was telling me about her driving test and everything. She's got a car, that's why she's not drinking. That doesn't make her boring. She knows what she wants in life. She's got a place at Cambridge. That's where I want to go.'

'Don't you have to be really clever to get in there?'

'Hmm.' Ava nodded.

'You'll get in, Ava, no problem. You don't have to do any work and you still get good grades. Unlike me.'

'You could do better if you put your mind to it. You're smart, you just can't be bothered. Tess likes you too, she told me.'

Lena shrugged; compliments were missiles to be lobbed away. 'Anyway, this is a party, Ava. Why are we talking about school grades and all that boring stuff? The music is great and we can drink whatever we like, go home whenever we want. And most importantly of all, there's a roomful of hot boys next door.'

'Yes, and Gareth.' Ava's shoulders slumped as if she was carrying a huge rucksack, weighing her down. Then she straightened. 'I've done it,' she said, smiling. 'We're over. I told Tess about him, and she was really understanding.'

Lena was sick of hearing about Miss Goody-Two-Shoes Tess.

'Gareth isn't happy, but I don't care,' said Ava. 'Let's go and get some more drinks, then come back in here and have some fun.'

'That's more like it,' Lena said. 'Let's try a drink we haven't had before. Have you ever tasted gin?'

Ava giggled. 'You know I haven't. I've only ever drunk with you. I've had Cinzano and martini and vodka. Oh, and wine, but that was at a dinner party my parents held when I was about ten.'

She remembered the leftover red liquid glimmering in the adults' discarded glasses. Drinking it had made them laugh like she'd never seen them laugh before, throwing their heads back, real belly laughs. When they were all off enjoying themselves doing a silly dance to some old records, she'd picked up a glass and taken a large sip. She'd almost choked, putting it back down quickly on the table. The liquid had tingled all the way down to her tummy, followed by a warm glow. She'd drunk the whole thing and spent the rest of the evening secretly giggling to herself under the table.

CHAPTER 24

Ava

Nobody notices as I slip back into the house, glancing at the kitchen clock as I head upstairs. It's almost ten; what if Ben isn't coming after all?

I lock the bathroom door behind me. Through the frosted glass of the small window the dark sky flashes with bursts of colour and loud popping noises from firework displays elsewhere. It's still early, I reassure myself; there's plenty of time for Ben to get here yet. A blast of red illuminates the window and I can't help thinking of roses, red roses gone bad. I shake the thought away. My worried eyes look back at me from the mirror and my cheeks are flushed. Ben always tells me I have beautiful eyes; he says the deep blue shade is unusual and unique. Why isn't he here?

Someone bangs on the door and I wash my hands with cold water before going back out. Fiona is waiting outside and we exchange a few pleasantries before I go into my bedroom. I check first under the bed for my phone, even though I know it's not there, then take everything out of my case again. I drag the duvet off the bed, followed by the sheet. A tissue falls on the floor, an old sock. Nothing here.

When I step out onto the landing, I see Martha coming upstairs. She motions to me to go back into my room.

'Lena's gone mad,' she says, pointing to Lena's room. 'Smashed a picture and everything. Maybe she's finally had a good look at herself and seen what I see. If I ever needed proof that there was something wrong with that woman, I've had plenty this evening. Mind you, what's going on in here?' She looks at the bed.

I shrug. 'I was looking for my phone. Lena's having a tough time with me leaving. Try and have some sympathy. This is a huge change for both of us.' I sit down on the bed and she pulls up a chair next to me. 'What were you even doing in her room?'

'Stupidly, I thought I'd try and have an adult conversation with her. That was a waste of time.'

'What did she say to you?'

She smooths her hair with her immaculate nails, dark polish against alabaster skin. 'The usual jealous diatribe. She hasn't changed. And that was after she'd chucked a few things around. Do you know what sparked this off?'

I take a deep breath. 'I let slip that Ben and I are getting married and I'm not planning on coming back. Ben will go mad; we'd agreed I wouldn't say anything until I was already there. He wanted us to make the announcement together. She's taking all this harder than I thought.'

'Congratulations, little sister. I'm thrilled for you. Will I get to meet him tonight, do you think?'

'I hope so. When I found out about the party, I thought he must be planning to surprise me by showing up and then announcing our engagement.'

'How romantic. Your eyes sparkle when you talk about him, so I hope he does come. Lena must want that for you too, surely?'

I nod, biting my lip. 'After everything … I think it's hard for her to let go. It's hard for both of us. When we were younger, we were so … entwined.'

She walks over to the window. 'Well she needs to realise it's time to move on. This is such a beautiful house, by the way. I see you got the best room. It's twice the size of Lena's.'

'She insisted I take this one. She knew I'd want Ben to stay over; she encouraged it.'

Martha looks sceptical. 'Is she dating anyone?'

I shake my head. 'None of her relationships have lasted very long. She likes to be in control and always says it's too much hassle trying to find someone who measures up to her ideal.'

'Did you know she has that newspaper cutting on her wall? She's still getting off on calling herself a hero.'

'She's always had that on display. I deliberately never look at it. I don't want to be reminded.' But the words dance in front of my eyes. *I did what anyone else would have done. Ava is my best friend and I was terrified of losing her.*

'If you ask me, she wants you never to forget how indebted to her you are. It's crazy; she has to let go for her own sanity, too. Honestly, Ava, she's a nutcase.'

'You've never liked her, though, have you? Let's not forget what's happened between us.'

'No, I haven't, I admit that, and I know it wasn't an easy time for any of us. I was grieving, you were in a terrible state and Mum and Dad inviting Lena to live with us was the worst thing that could have happened as far as I was concerned. She was always there, glued to your side, and she wouldn't let me near you. I missed you. We were so close when we were younger; you were my little shadow.'

A lump slips into my throat. 'It wasn't deliberate. Think about how it must have been for her, too. Being ripped from her family, no matter how dysfunctional they were, was hard. And I wasn't there for her either, too devastated by what I'd done.'

'Maybe not, but it felt intentional. Heading off to university saved me, but I'm sorry it ended with that argument.'

'Me too. You were so angry.' My voice shakes as I remember the fear that gripped me when she turned on me, my throat seizing up, rendering me speechless.

'I intended to get back in touch, but somehow Lena was always there.'

She spits out the name and a sense of hopelessness washes over me. That anger is forever simmering inside her. How are they ever going to reconcile?

'Quite frankly, her still being here is weird, but I swallowed my pride tonight and tried to clear the air with her. I hoped we could agree to a truce, to tolerate one another for your sake. I want to be back in touch with you. Life's too short.' She flicks her hair back and I see the young Martha in the sad expression that momentarily crosses her face.

'Is something wrong?' I ask.

'Why does something have to be wrong? I miss you, you idiot, that's all.' Her cheeks flush pink. 'I've been wanting to speak to you for a while, and when Mum told me you were leaving the country, it seemed like fate.'

'Speak to me about what? If you haven't forgiven me, then nothing has changed.'

'Of course I've forgiven you. Obviously I'll never forget, but you were young, and I was young too and didn't understand. You would never talk about what happened and I needed that, can't you see? I was hurting so much, and despite everything, despite how I felt about you, I needed my sister. I missed you, but I couldn't get near you because of Lena. You let her come between us, and she's still here. I've fantasised about her disappearing so many times, about being a part of your life again. I knew she would never let that happen. But now, finally, you're getting away from her. That's why I'm here, why I can talk about what happened. I can only do it because you're going, do you see?'

A sensation of warmth fills my body. Martha is voicing the words I've wanted to hear for so long. She forgives me.

'That means so much, Martha,' I tell her.

She leans forward to hear my voice, which is barely a whisper, and then we're hugging, my senses overloaded with her familiarity and the smell of her skin, the fragrance of fresh rose petals.

I sit back, trying to hide the shudder that ricochets through me, Lena's suspicions about Martha flitting into my mind, spoiling the moment. Could my sister have sent the roses? Is she the one behind all this?

'I don't want to talk about what happened,' I say. 'I don't even remember much. I never have. I've had therapy and all sorts, but nothing will jog my memory. Maybe it's blocked out for a reason and my mind is trying to keep me safe. That's why I'm leaving. I want to put it all behind me. Ben doesn't know anything about it and I don't want him to know. I want to start over. Properly.' I flash her a warning look.

'That isn't going to work, Ava. What happened is part of who you are. You have to deal with things, not run away from them. Don't you think having Lena around all the time makes it even more difficult to forget? She's a constant reminder of that time. Far better to be honest with Ben before you start your life together. Relationships are based on trust. You're dooming it to failure otherwise.' She moves over to sit next to me on the bed. 'You know, I could see how ill you were at the time, no matter what you'd done and how much I hated you for it. You were traumatised. I wanted to help you. Despite everything, you're my sister, you always will be. But Lena isn't part of our family, no matter how hard she pretends.'

She's got Lena all wrong. She's always come down hard on her, doesn't see the lovely side of her that I see. I open my mouth to defend my friend, but Martha carries on.

'I was so pleased you were going to university, finally getting away from her, and then she was always there too. I couldn't believe it. Stopping you from studying, never letting you forget your past. Couldn't you see it?' She smiles to herself. 'Mind you, how could you? She even managed to bewitch our parents. What does Ben think of her?'

I sigh. 'She hasn't bewitched anybody. Mum and Dad are kind people, that's all. Don't forget they were devastated too and were trying to do a good thing amongst so much bad. As for Ben …' I pat my hair, turning away from her, searching for the right words to explain another of Lena's difficult relationships. 'Obviously they've met loads of times, but at best I guess they tolerate each other. To be honest, they both want me all to themselves.'

'See, she's doing it again. It's normal for your partner to want you to himself – within reason, of course – but friends are different.'

'Maybe.' I stretch my arms out. 'It's so complicated. All I want is an easy life.'

'Hopefully this move will achieve that. Where is Ben anyway? You said he was supposed to be here.'

'I know. I'm worried that something's happened to him. That's why I'm trying to find my phone.'

'Well, Lena got a text from him when I arrived. I saw his name.'

'A text? But she doesn't have his number,' I say.

'I guess it could have been an email. Whatever it was, she's in touch with him. What has she said about where he is?'

'She said he arrived in London hours ago. She's got me thinking he doesn't want to be here.'

'Don't be silly, of course he wants to be here – he's your fiancé. I really am thrilled for you, you know. I reckon Mum and Dad have given up hope of me ever getting married.'

'Thanks. I can't wait for you to see my ring.' I twist the phantom ring on my finger, imagine it sparkling in the light. 'Would you like to see it now? I've got it here.'

'Let's try and get hold of Ben first, set your mind at rest. What's his number?'

'I don't know. It's written down in my address book, which is at home. We could call Mum and ask her for it.'

'They've gone out for dinner. They won't be back for ages yet. I'll text her. She might have his number on her; if not, she can check when she gets back. And I'll help you look for your phone. But let's get a drink first. I stuck the champagne back in the fridge after the distraction earlier. Someone's probably guzzled it by now, but you never know, it might still be in there.' She pulls her phone out and taps out a text. 'As soon as I get his number, you can message him and ask him where he is and how long he's going to be.'

I'm following my sister downstairs when she suddenly stops and I bump into her. The scent of her Chanel perfume is so familiar, I'm overwhelmed by a rush of emotion. It feels incredible that I haven't seen her for so many years.

'Who is that woman?' she asks, indicating Kate, who is talking to someone by the front door.

'She's the partner of a guy from work.'

'Friend of Lena's?'

'No, not as far as I know.'

'Well they were looking pretty chummy earlier, chatting in a corner.' Martha carries on downstairs. 'She was looking at me as if she knew me, but that happens a lot.'

'How does it feel being recognised?' I ask.

She shrugs, but a smile plays around her mouth. 'Oh, you get used to it. Eyes straight ahead and walk purposefully if you're not in the mood for chit-chat; if you look like you're in a hurry to get somewhere important, most people get the message pretty quickly.' She laughs. 'They get short shrift if they don't.'

As we approach the living room, where Madonna's 'Holiday' is playing at full blast, I take Martha's arm, inhaling the rosy scent of her body lotion.

'I have to ask you something. It might sound weird, but it's important.'

'OK,' she says, her lips flickering into a smile. 'Sounds intriguing.'

'Have you sent me any roses?'

'Today? Or ever?' She shrugs her elegant shoulders. 'Whichever it is, the answer is no. Should I have? Our relationship has been somewhat strained for the past few years, to put it mildly. Would a rose have helped?'

She raises an eyebrow and laughs, and I do too – she always could make me laugh with her unique brand of humour – but the thought of the dark roses soon wipes the smile from my face.

'Far more likely to be from a secret admirer, wouldn't you think? Ben, or Gaz.' She rolls her eyes as she uses the pet name she assigned to Gareth, which he's always hated. 'Why am I not surprised he's still hanging around? Have you asked him?'

'These aren't normal roses …' An image of dark petals bruised like flesh stops me mid sentence. 'They're horrible – black, unnatural. Coloured deliberately. They carry some kind of message. I've been getting them in the post for years, but there's never any indication who's sending them. Gareth brought a rose with him when he arrived this evening. Lena was going to ask him if he was responsible for the others, but I haven't had a chance to find out yet what he said.'

'Well there you go. It sounds weird, just like Gareth. Although isn't he more of a computer geek? I would have thought he'd be far more likely to harass someone online. Is it that important? Forget it, is my advice. Enjoy the party; it sounds like everyone else is.'

'If Lena hasn't got round to it, then I'll ask him myself.' My arm brushes against a jacket someone has left over the banister, and I yank my arm away, the soft corduroy reminding me of a black petal stroking my skin. I wish I'd never raised the subject. 'I'll catch you up in a minute,' I say. I'm no longer in the mood for champagne.

The hallway looks untidy, and I move the jacket and hang it on the coat rack out of sight. Someone has left an empty glass on the table, and a copy of the local paper, which nobody ever reads, has been put through the letter box. I pick it up, but as I go to add it to the pile of post set aside for recycling, I'm consumed by the feeling that something isn't quite right, and I take a closer look.

A face stares out from under the lurid headline; the photo of the serious-looking girl with her pixie cut is as familiar to me as my own school photo hanging in the living room, in which I grin through a gap in my teeth at whoever comes to visit. That photo is annoying, but this one ignites a flame of fear inside me. What does it mean? Why now?

It takes me a moment to realise exactly what I'm looking at. It's only when I take in the headline – *CEDAR HIGH SCHOOL TEENAGE HERO, see page 5* – that I seek out the date of the newspaper, my pulse racing as I know what I will find. *Thursday 21 February 2005*. I meet the serious eyes of the girl I used to know and feel a bolt of sadness.

A draught blows through the gap under the front door and the hairs on my arms stand upright. Questions come thick and fast like raindrops: who put this through the door? Why do they want to remind me of what happened thirteen years ago? I scan the paper as if the answers can be found hidden between the lines on the front pages. This is no copy; it's an original. Somebody has kept this article for a reason.

An unexpected burst of noise from the doorbell makes my heart hammer hard against my ribs. I shove the newspaper to the bottom of the recycling box and smooth my hair from my sweaty forehead, my hands fumbling with the catch of the door as I pull it open. *Go away*, I want to say to whoever is standing there; *please leave* to the throng of people in the living room. I want to see every last person depart, then bolt the door behind them, shutting them all out. But I don't. Instead I pin a smile on my mouth, the same false, shaky smile I have been wearing for all these years. I stand firm against the blast of cold air that rushes at me and pretend to welcome yet another guest who may be wishing to do me harm.

CHAPTER 25

Lena

The smoke from outside is bugging me, so I close the window, so hard it vibrates. *She's getting married.* The words spin around my mind. After a while, I hear voices out on the landing, Martha's distinctive too-loud voice and a quieter one. Ava. A door closes. I bash my fist into the wall. Martha isn't supposed to be here. Her Chanel perfume lingers in my room, expensive, sickly. I feel violated. This is my home, my life, my mess. *Was* my home, I remind myself. As of tomorrow, I'm officially home*less*. Homeless in London means people huddling in doorways, shivering under thick jackets and woolly hats, eyes wary behind cigarettes. Homeless can't be me. Sofa surfing, they call it. I regret not taking one of the flats I've been to see, but none of them lived up to this place, to the memories Ava and I share. I don't want to think about the new memories she's about to make, without me, and with Ben. I check my phone, but there's nothing from him. He's my last chance.

I clear a space on the floor and sit down, wincing as something digs into my hand. A piece of glass from the mirror, a nasty edge piercing my flesh. Next to it lies my framed article. I pick it up and hold it tight against my chest. Not being the most careful of people, I'm surprised I haven't broken it before now; it must be at least twelve years old.

Back then, Sue encouraged me to be proud of myself, to shout about my accomplishments. Having a mother who walked out when I was so young and a father who showed no interest in me didn't exactly fill me with confidence. Sue was a proper mother to her daughters. And later, once she got past her initial suspicion, a mother figure to me. She and David instilled self-belief in their girls, convincing them that they could take on the world. They grew up so differently to me. All I have of my mother is a photograph. A few not so great memories. A different dad might have kept her memory alive for me, but not our father; he never mentioned her again after she left, and sold everything we had to feed his drinking habit. She had good reason to leave, I imagine.

Blood bubbles on my hand and I grab a wad of tissue from the dressing table and hold it over the cut. With my right hand I remove the cracked glass from the frame and take out the newspaper article. The paper is brittle and yellow; it's the only copy I have. I'm sure I could find it online, but it wouldn't be the same. I held this piece of paper in my hand when my life changed. It's symbolic. I almost know the words by heart.

Lena Baker, 16, from Cedar High School was today hailed a hero by friends and neighbours as her quick thinking saved the life of her friend.

Fifteen-year-old Ava Thomas had been drinking at a party and left in a distressed state, running into the path of a car. The car, driven by fellow Cedar pupil Teresa Davies, appeared to swerve in a failed attempt to avoid her and hit a tree, the impact turning the car on its side. Seventeen-year-old Teresa was killed instantly. Joyce Parrott, 62, a neighbour, who witnessed the scene from her front room, gave her version of events. 'I was about to draw the curtains when I heard a screech and a thump and saw the wrecked car outside. I rushed out to help and saw a girl attempting to resuscitate another young girl who was lying in the road. She looked in a bad way. I called an ambulance and then waited with the girl, who told me her name was Lena. The ambulance arrived very quickly and the paramedics took over. Lena was taken away to be checked over, but all she was concerned about was her friend. She saved her life without a doubt. Such a brave girl.'

Police are asking anyone who was in the area or had been at the party in Carisbrooke Close to come forward to help them with enquiries. Lena, who is now recovering at home, said, 'I did what anyone else would have done. Ava is my best friend and I was terrified of losing her.'

The head of Cedar High expressed his condolences to the Davies family and said, 'The whole community is devastated at the loss of one of our sixth-formers. Teresa was an outstanding student who achieved nine A-star grades at GCSE and was expected to take up a place at Cambridge next year to study English. That evening she was celebrating passing her driving test, and had her whole future in front of her. A memorial service will be taking place sometime later in the year.'

Fellow student Ava Thomas is in a critical condition in hospital and her parents were too upset to comment. Robert Johnson, Ava's uncle, asked that the family be left alone at this time as they wait for Ava to recover. 'She's a lovely girl and we're all devastated and praying for her recovery. We owe a lot to the bravery of her friend.'

The scene is alive in my mind – the screeching of the tyres and the blood mixing with gravel on the road; the warmth of Mrs Parrott's hand on my back as she encouraged me to keep up the compression on Ava's chest. Without me, Ava would have ended up dead, just like Tess. Why can't Martha see that? She could have lost her sister as well as her best friend, but she's never even acknowledged that fact. I pick up a piece of glass and hold my index finger against it, enjoying the pain. I bet Martha's never suffered like this, with her swanky showbiz life, never experienced pain likes it's a piece of broken glass jabbing into your heart. It's how I feel about Ava going.

A shrill sound breaks through my self-pity. It's the doorbell, a long, insistent ring like earlier. I scramble to my feet, unable to stand the sight of this mess any longer. It reminds me of my room when I was a kid. A crumpled bed surrounded by piles of clothes, clean mixed in with dirty, no room for anything else. But at least I could lock the door from the inside back then, the only way to keep myself safe from my father and his violent moods.

The staircase is free of guests, and I run down fast, anxious now to rejoin the party. Ava is standing in the hallway holding an empty glass, staring at a pile of junk mail. Martha is nowhere to be seen. It would be too much to hope that she's left already.

Ava jumps when she notices me. The news of the engagement hovers between us, an unwelcome presence. 'What are you doing?' I ask.

A peal of laughter bursts from the lounge as a man comes out and charges up the stairs.

'No time to chat,' he says. 'I'm a bit desperate.'

Ava seems oblivious to what is going on.

'Why are you staring at the post instead of in there enjoying yourself?' I say. 'Has Martha upset you?' I won't let Martha spoil this evening for either of us.

'No,' she says. 'But I need my phone. I'm worried about Ben.'

'He'll be here.'

'You keep saying that, but will he?'

'I'm sure he will. We have to think positive. Come on.' I take her arm. 'Let's go and join your friends.'

She shakes my hand off. 'It's not really Ben I'm worrying about; more the fact that my phone has disappeared. And the roses, of course. Have you spoken to Gareth?'

'Yes. He denied it and seemed genuinely surprised. He said he found the rose outside.'

'Ah, so it could have been the one you chucked in the bin earlier. That makes me feel slightly better. But my phone isn't the only thing I've lost.' She clenches her fists at her sides. 'I can't find my passport.'

'Isn't all your stuff at your mum's?'

'Most of it, but I'm sure I kept my passport with me. It's kind of stupid, but I like having it close by. It makes it all seem more real somehow. But I've unpacked my case twice now, and it isn't there.'

Her words wind me and it's my fists that are clenched now. She can't wait to get away. *Accept it, Lena.*

'You've left some stuff on the shelf in the kitchen, don't forget. Books and some paperwork. It's probably there. Why don't you forget about it for the next few hours? I want you to enjoy this party.'

'You're right, it's bound to be there. God, I'm being selfish. You must think I'm a right spoilt brat. But I need to check so I can stop worrying about it. You know how I like everything to be organised. I'll take that stuff upstairs and have a quick look through it. Then I promise I'll dance and drink myself silly.'

The volume in the lounge is deafening in contrast with the quiet of the hall; in here, the babble of conversation competes with the music, glasses clink against one another and the heat is stifling. Martha stands at the far end talking to three women, who look as if they are in thrall to her. She notices us going past, and I follow Ava into the kitchen, avoiding her gaze.

'Ava, there you are,' one of her friends says. 'We were just talking about New York. When are you actually leaving?'

'In two days' time,' Ava says, but she's looking towards the shelf where her possessions are stacked. 'Give me a few minutes, I've just got to sort something out. I'll be right back.'

She stands on tiptoe to reach the shelf, which is slightly out of her reach.

'Hey, let me.' Kate, who is at least six foot tall, comes to her aid. 'What is it you want from here?' Her presence makes me feel jittery, and I move away from her.

'The whole pile,' Ava says. 'I just need to take it upstairs.'

Kate lifts the stack of books and paperwork down in one easy motion. 'I'll take it up for you,' she says. 'It's your party, it's the least I can do to help the guest of honour. Where do you want it?'

'Upstairs, first room on the left at the top of the stairs,' Ava says. Kate looks at me as she leads the way. Our eyes meet and her smile flickers at me. It's one of those unpleasant smiles that looks like it hides a mouthful of rotten teeth. It sends anxiety coursing through me.

CHAPTER 26
2005

Ava and Lena went back into the sitting room, where people were dancing. Someone had turned the lights down and the teenagers had lost their inhibitions, letting their bodies follow the dance track that was booming out. In the semi-darkness, Ava could see a couple canoodling on the sofa. Danny was in the middle of a large group. His dance moves were fluid and unselfconscious. She wished she could be like that. He was so good-looking, and the thought gave her a shock. She looked around for Lena, as if her friend was able to read her guilty thoughts. But Lena was chatting to a boy from school at the other end of the room.

Suddenly Jon appeared at her side. 'Hey, Ava, do you want to dance?'

She nodded. At first she was shy, anxious about the way her limbs were moving, but Jon chatted to her over the music – shouting to make himself heard, which made them both laugh – and she quickly stopped worrying about what she looked like. The alcohol in her body made everything appear lighter, brighter. She was laughing at something Jon had said when Gareth appeared at her side. From nowhere he moved across to Jon and punched him. Jon fell against a girl behind him and someone shouted. Ava grabbed Gareth's arm.

'What are you doing?'

'It's him, isn't it? He's the reason you've dumped me.'

Ava wished she could fade into the walls, evaporate from the scene. Everybody was staring in her direction. A circle of onlookers focused on Gareth, who was breathing heavily. Then Danny appeared.

'We don't want any bother, Gareth, mate. I think you should come outside and cool down.'

Danny had a deep tone to his voice and an air of authority. He was the kind of person people listened to. Ava let out a gasp of relief as Gareth disappeared with him.

'Are you OK?' she asked Jon, who looked stunned.

'Yeah. What was all that about? Is he your boyfriend?'

'He was, up until this evening.'

Jon rubbed his head. 'He took it well, then.' They both laughed. 'Let me get us some more drinks.'

Chatter filled the air again, voices battling over the music, and Ava relaxed into an empty armchair.

Danny appeared at her side. 'Are you OK?'

She moved to get up and he placed his hand on her arm. The unexpected gesture made her instinctively glance around to see where Lena was.

'No, stay there.' He knelt down beside her.

'Where's Gareth?' Ava asked.

'He left.'

'Just like that?'

'He didn't say anything, went all silent on me, as if he was embarrassed. I thought you two were going out?'

Ava was amazed he'd even noticed her. She recounted what had happened earlier that evening. 'He saw me talking to Jon, but I'm not the slightest bit interested in him. We just hit it off.'

'You wouldn't get very far with Jon anyway; he's not attracted to girls, if you get what I'm saying.'

It took a minute before his words made sense to Ava, blood rushing to her cheeks when she understood. She was always the last to catch on; Lena usually had to fill her in on everything. But that explained why Jon was so easy to chat to. She hadn't felt him sizing her up, judging whether she was worth talking to based on how sexy or easy he thought she was, like a lot of boys so obviously did.

Danny watched her reaction and they both laughed. Her mind had been racing before he came over, but his words had soothed her. He pulled up a stool and she ended up telling him about her relationship with Gareth and how a weight had been lifted from her. After a while, they rejoined the dancing, and when a slow track came on and Danny pulled her to him, it felt natural to move with him and the music, inhaling his aftershave, which smelt of pine trees, and feeling his warm hands on her back. As they rotated on the dance floor, she saw Lena in the doorway, arms folded and a sour expression on her face.

CHAPTER 27

Ava

Kate leads the way up the stairs, striding ahead on her long legs. She has to be over six feet; I'm five eight and I don't normally feel small, but she's lean and athletic, graceful in the way she carries herself. She stops outside my bedroom door.

'Where do you want these?'

'On the bed is fine, thanks. It's just something I need to find. It won't take a minute. Thanks so much for bringing them up.'

She hovers, not leaving as I expect her to.

'Need any more help?' she asks.

'Thanks, but I'm fine.'

'Can I ask you something?'

'Of course,' I say, although I'm itching to look for my passport.

'Why are you leaving?'

'I'm moving abroad. Didn't ... sorry, I can't remember your partner's name, but didn't he tell you?'

She laughs. 'No, I mean why are you leaving this house?'

'I guess I have to.' *Strange question.*

'It's a gorgeous place. Is Lena moving too?'

'Yes, we both are. The lease is coming to an end. We could have renewed it, but as I was moving, she decided to leave too.'

'I'd be interested in moving in, but I guess it's too late now?'

'I don't know. It might be worth mentioning it to Lena.'

'I'll do that. She must be gutted. You guys seem so close.'

'We are. You should definitely ask her, though. It can't hurt.'

'Yeah, I think I will.' She leaves the room and I hear her running down the stairs as if she's taking them two at a time.

I close the door behind her and with feverish fingers go through the pile to see what's here. A sinking feeling tells me it's a pointless exercise, but a small bead of hope keeps me looking. It's a random collection of items that wouldn't fit in the car earlier: a few recipe books, which I shake to check nothing has slipped inside them, a couple of folders containing work from my degree, and a box file. I pause for a moment at the sight of my final dissertation, remembering the relief I felt when I handed it in – in retrospect, my time at university was too close to what had happened, and I'm amazed I came out of it with any kind of degree at all. Lena helped me through it, though, like always.

A shout and a bang from downstairs remind me I need to hurry. Fear trickles through my veins as I force myself to confront the possibility that my passport's disappearance is connected to the roses and the newspaper that was pushed through the letter box. I should probably have kept it for evidence instead of discarding it as if it was burning my fingers. It might as well have been. My mind races ahead into fantastical possibilities – what if Ben has been harmed by whoever is sending the roses, to stop me from going away with him? My dreams feel precarious right now.

Pushing the thoughts away, I pick up the last item in the pile, the box file. Inside are some loose photographs and a photo album. I recall Mum filling it for me one evening, fed up with me shoving all my photos in a drawer. She organised them in chronological order from my university graduation onwards.

An almighty crack grabs my attention, and I look towards the window, where a green firework bursts upwards, sending a trail of sparkles through the inky sky. I turn back to the album, and as I open it, a bolt of fear shoots through me. In the first photo, of me at my graduation, my face has been scratched out. My fingers fumble at the pages, slippery with sweat, as I turn them one by one, afraid of what I might see. Everyone else who appears in the photos is looking back at the camera, face captured for posterity. Unlike mine, which has been obliterated in every shot. I slam the album shut with trembling hands. Who would do this?

Over by the window, I fold my arms tightly, willing the shaking to lessen. Watching the bonfire, I'm mesmerised by the orange tongues of flame that flicker at the sky. Somebody wants to do me harm, I'm convinced of it. The energy of the fire emboldens me, and suddenly it feels imperative that I keep the newspaper I found as evidence, otherwise nobody will take me seriously. I run downstairs and snatch the pile of papers from the recycling box, then hurry back up, my feet pounding in time to the music that fills the house. I pick up the photo album and shove it under the bed together with the recycling.

Footsteps sound on the stairs and I hear Martha calling my name. In that moment I make a snap decision. I have no idea who is doing these things to me, which means I must trust no one. Until Ben arrives, I'll keep this to myself. So what if I can't find my passport? There are ways round it. My priority now is finding out who is doing this and stopping them.

'I've had a text from Mum,' Martha says as I close the door of my room behind me. 'She's got Ben's number back at the house, but she won't be home for a couple of hours yet. As soon as she's back, she'll let us know.'

Lena appears at the bottom of the stairs.

'Ava, you have to come, it's urgent.'

What now? I ignore Martha muttering under her breath, and race downstairs.

'What is it?'

Lena puts her arm around my waist and leads me into the living room, where the guests have split into little clusters. She guides me over to the sofa and we sink down into it.

'Nothing,' she says, wiping sweat from her forehead. 'Imagine this was your wedding. Think of me as the chief bridesmaid. It's my role to make sure you're enjoying yourself at all times. It's a party, for God's sake.' She moves her shoulders in time to the catchy music, and we watch a small group who were sitting on the floor getting up to dance, chatting as they do so. I feel a rush of warmth towards everyone who is here.

'You're right,' I say, and I pull Lena into a hug, feeling the heat of her body against my cold one. Fake it till you make it – that's what they say, isn't it? 'Let's get some drinks.'

'I get it that your sister is here and it's a big deal,' Lena says as we wind our way in and out of the revellers. 'But you'll have the rest of your life to catch up. I'm sure she'll be inviting herself over to New York the minute you arrive. Live in the moment, that's my motto.'

In the kitchen, we opt for gin and tonics. I go to mention Kate and her interest in moving in, but Lena starts speaking at the same moment.

'Remember the first time you tried vodka?'

'Don't. I had no idea about measures back then – no wonder I threw up afterwards. That's why I stick to gin nowadays.'

'I'd do it all again, you know.'

'Would you? I wouldn't.'

'Not that …' Our eyes meet. 'You and me, I mean.'

I sip at my gin. 'Well obviously.'

Lena's eyes have the misty sheen they always take on when she's reminiscing.

'We're enjoying ourselves, remember,' I warn her, ignoring the image of my scratched-out face that keeps jumping into my head.

'I've had this idea,' she says. She looks hopeful now, and takes a drink before speaking.

'Oh yes?'

'Let me come to New York with you. You thought I was joking before, didn't you? Well I wasn't; I couldn't be more serious. You'll have plenty of time to discuss it with Ben when he arrives. I've already been checking out the job situation, courses I could take.'

'I knew you were serious,' I say.

What with everything that's been happening this evening and the way I've been feeling, having someone to share the move with appeals, certainly, especially given how much Lena has been there for me. But I can see Ben's face, the look he gets whenever I mention Lena, the lines that appear in his forehead, the way he pushes his floppy hair out of his eyes as if it's driving him mad. It's impossible. What I need is a new life, new friends. Words are racing around in my head as I pick out the right ones to say without hurting her. She means well, after all.

'It's tempting, but not a good idea in the long run. Ben wouldn't like it, for one thing.'

'Why wouldn't he? You don't know until you ask him.'

'It wouldn't work,' I say.

Lena flinches, and immediately I regret being so blunt. But for how long can I keep sugar-coating this?

'Have you heard from him yet?' I ask.

She shakes her head. 'I asked what flight he was getting and he said it was better I didn't know so we don't mess up the surprise. He's arrived in London, that's all I know.' She pauses, smooths her dress down. 'I didn't want to have to tell you this, but I sensed a reluctance on his part. I expected him here by now. I just put it down to him not liking me very much.'

'Of course he does,' I say.

'Ava, we both know that's not true.'

I automatically play with my ring finger, but stop when a hurt look crosses her face.

'Come on, there's no need to pretend, not now. Last Easter, we'd planned to go over together and then you suddenly changed your mind after speaking to him. We were both so excited, but you decided it was a bad idea right after that conversation.'

'He's a guy, it's just a man thing. He doesn't understand my need for a close female friend now that I've got him. He's my partner, Lena …' I almost say *fiancé* but stop myself in time. 'I don't want my friendship with you to cause any friction between us.'

'I knew it.' She presses her lips together, frowning.

'Don't let it spoil the party.'

'Yeah, right. Let's check out what's going on outside,' she says, but she won't meet my eyes.

I want to tell her I didn't mean to hurt her, but Steph appears at the back door before I can get the words out.

'How's it going out there?' Lena asks. We all look towards the bonfire, which glows in the dark, illuminating the shadowy figures standing around it.

Steph wipes her forehead, leaving a sooty mark. 'Phew, I need some water.' She fills a glass with tap water and drinks it down in one go. 'I needed that. The potatoes are cooking nicely and we're gearing up for the display. We've got an hour until the fireworks – we're going to let them off at midnight. But my part is done for the moment. Felix is on bonfire duty for the next half-hour. Dance with me, Ava?' She beseeches me with her eyes.

'Fancy a dance, Lena?' I ask.

'No, you go. I'll stay out here for a bit, check the drink supplies, make sure we've got enough out. I'll join you in a bit.' She's still not looking at me, and the muscles in her neck are tensed.

'OK, come and find us after. By the way, try and talk to Kate,' I call back to her. 'She's got a proposition for you.'

Now she's staring at me, her body rigid, and I don't understand the look of terror in her eyes.

CHAPTER 28

Lena

Kate isn't in the living room, so I check out the kitchen, my pulse racing, bemused at Ava's comment and anxious to find out what's going on. Steph's interruption was bad timing. Ava was tempted by my plan, I'm sure of it – I could see her hesitation. A little more persuasion is all that's needed. She was so close to seeing what a good idea it would be for me to join her.

Out in the garden, the fairy lights strung up in the trees twinkle, and the cold air blowing through the back door is welcome now that it's so warm in the house. I refill my glass with some wine from an opened bottle and take the rest of it outside, looking for Kate. Smoke fills the air and I breathe in the woody smell. Pete is sitting on the bench at the far end of the garden. As I head towards him, I turn to look back at the house, spotting that Kate has just gone into the kitchen. Pete looks in the same direction.

'I see Kate's here,' he says.

'I was just looking for her. Did you invite her?'

'Not me. I try and keep out of her way. She's a bit of a head case.'

'What makes you say that?'

'Let's say she took our break-up a little harder than I expected. Bombarded me with texts.'

'Hmm. And I wonder what she'd say about you.'

He grins. 'Pour us a glass of that wine, will you, and sit down.'

I lower myself next to him on the bench and he sips at the wine. The music carries from the house, floating on the breeze towards us. The lights are on next door and I wonder if it's too loud, but it's hard to care. Each time I remember that we have to move out tomorrow, that Ava's leaving me, she's been hiding things from me, it's like everything that matters in my life is swept aside. Nothing makes sense without her.

'Why are you here?' I ask. After everything Ava's told me about Pete, I have no idea why he'd want to come to her party.

'Hey.' Kate walks over to us, interrupting, her breath white against the dark surrounding us. Over by the bonfire, Felix and a couple of others look to be getting the fireworks ready. I get up and wander over to warm my hands, and she follows.

'Ava says—'

'Bloody hell, it's freezing,' Pete says, appearing next to us.

I move closer to the bonfire. I must look ridiculous in my clingy party dress, shivering in the cold November night.

'I can smell the potatoes cooking,' he adds. 'It's making me hungry.'

'Not too long to wait now,' Felix says, throwing more wood on the fire. 'There's a tight schedule for this evening, so I'm afraid you'll have to wait until Steph gives the go-ahead to eat. Everything must run smoothly or else my life won't be worth living. She says you've got another surprise planned too, Lena.'

'Oh yeah?' Pete looks at me.

'Everybody will just have to wait and see,' I say, watching Felix poking at the foil-wrapped potatoes with the long fork he's holding, spreading the burning wood evenly, jumping back as the fire spits at him. Something clangs as the fork hits metal.

'What's that?' he says, leaning towards the fire. He pokes around and lifts the fork, a metal frame dangling from it. It glows with a blue tinge. 'I wonder how that got there.'

'Weird,' Pete says. 'Maybe it was already on the ground.'

Felix shakes his head. 'I don't remember seeing it.'

'Doesn't really matter as long as the food's cooking,' Pete says, and Felix laughs.

Pete slings the frame away from the bonfire and it lands near my feet. I take a closer look. It's rectangular, and has a dent in one corner. Despite the raging heat of the fire, my blood runs cold. I know exactly what this is.

'I'm going to the bathroom,' I say to nobody in particular, my voice trembling. I hurry into the house, adrenalin firing me up as I speed through the lounge.

'Great party,' a man says, and I throw a thank you at whoever it was without stopping.

I'm hoping I'm wrong; I'm praying as I rush up the stairs. But in my room, the broken glass from the mirror is in a heap on the floor where I left it, but the newspaper clipping that I have treasured for so many years is gone. I picture the burning paper shrivelling as the heat devours it, the frame the only bit left behind. I try not to care – the words are imprinted in my memory anyway – but I can't help it. The article marks the turning point in my life; the moment that changed everything. Who would be trying to hurt me like this? A face looms in my mind against the burning background.

I open my bedroom window and lean out, breathing in the smoky air. Pete and Kate have moved back to the bench, and Felix is sipping a beer, his garden fork leaning against the tree. The flames pick up the dull sheen of the metal frame discarded on the trampled grass. Tears spring into my eyes and I sniff them back.

I watch as a few people emerge into the garden, but I don't see who I'm looking for. I know exactly who is behind this and I won't let her get away with it. It has to be Martha. How dare she sneer at me? Why shouldn't I feel proud of myself? I saved my best friend's life – her sister – and for some reason she is punishing me for it. I clench and unclench my fists, trying to calm my breathing, to ease the tight feeling in my chest. Sue and David taking me in when I was sixteen was the best thing that could have happened to me. Whenever I think about how my life could have turned out, Sue's kindness and her belief in me feel like warm hands wrapped around mine.

I close my bedroom door and head downstairs. I need a drink. A balloon pops, followed by a shriek. The music suddenly stops. The party can't end yet. It's not even midnight. We have food and fireworks, and nothing will stop that; whoever is trying to sabotage this party won't win.

I race into the living room, where Ava stands surrounded by a group of people whose expressions I can't read. But the emotion on Ava's face is clear to see. Her mouth is slightly open and her eyes are wide. She looks terrified.

CHAPTER 29
2005

Lena stood in the doorway, her heart pounding in her chest. Ava was dancing with Danny. How could she? She watched the way her best friend leaned into the boy she fancied, how he ran his hands up and down her back. Danny was oblivious to everything in the room apart from Ava; she could tell by the glassy look in his eyes. They were rocking slowly in a circle, and eventually Ava was facing her. She saw the moment Ava registered her presence and stiffened, momentarily interrupting the rhythm of their bodies moving in unison.

Lena twisted her hands together, unable to tear her eyes away. Boys were only ever after one thing, she knew that; everyone knew that. She had made a special effort to look her best for Danny; she'd shaved her legs and smothered herself in an intoxicating Clarins body lotion she'd found in Ava's mum's room. Clarins was one of those brands with expensive-looking women guarding their beauty counter, sending undesirables away with their painted-on eyebrows and over-made-up stares. Lena had made herself look as good as she could for Danny, only to have Ava take her place. But Ava wasn't interested in him, surely? She was meant to be her best friend. Her sister.

She and Ava had a connection, despite their differences. But Ava was drunk, didn't know what she was doing. She was so naïve. She had a loving family, a family who looked after her in ways Lena had never known. She had everything, and yet she'd gone and stolen Danny from right under Lena's nose.

CHAPTER 30

Ava

'That looked a bit intense back there,' Steph says as we make our way into the lounge. 'Did I interrupt something?'

'Yeah … Lena was talking about coming with me to New York. She's found a course and everything.' Maybe I could tell Steph about the photos, how someone wants to obliterate me.

'She's got to be joking?'

'She definitely isn't. At first I wasn't sure about the idea, but if I'm honest, it would make things easier for me.'

'Seriously? Don't be silly. You're going to be with Ben; neither of you wants her tagging along like a gooseberry, do you? I know how close you two are, but do you think it's healthy?'

I shrug. She wouldn't understand. 'We go back a long way, we've been through so much together. It's complicated.' I can't tell her the whole story – no one knows the whole story.

'Is everything OK with you and Ben?' Steph asks hesitantly.

'Of course.' I twist a strand of hair that has fallen free.

'Sure? You don't sound convinced.'

'It's just a small thing. Last time we spoke, he sounded a little bit strange, as if he had something on his mind, but when I asked him about it, he said everything was fine. But you know when you get a feeling about something?' I recall his face on the screen, the darkness under his eyes, which seemed unable to connect to mine. Ordinarily he'd lie on his bed to Skype me, hand propping up his head, lazy grin making me melt inside. Last time, though, he was perched on the edge of his sofa, laptop wobbling on his knees, his mouth a serious line.

Steph leans close to me, the music so loud she is practically shouting in my ear.

'It'll be fine. You're making a big change to your relationship and you're both bound to be nervous. That's all. And if you're struggling at first, having Lena there won't make it easier; it will add a whole load of new stress. You talk about Gareth being obsessed with you; don't you think she is too?'

'No, it isn't like that.' But I can't explain – how can I? This surprise party full of my friends is all down to Lena; even talking about her like this makes me feel disloyal.

'Come on,' Steph says. 'Forget all that crap, let's dance.'

Her mood is infectious, and I follow her into the living room, throwing myself into the rhythm of the music, shutting out my chattering thoughts. A couple of other people join us. I move in a slow circle, looking at every part of the room, taking it all in, remembering when Lena originally brought me into this house, her surprise. She did good that time.

I'm hot and sweaty, and I pause to grab my glass. I remember the champagne Martha brought with her and wonder where she is. Moving my body in time with the music, I swivel to take in the other end of the room, where a couple are sitting on the sofa that Lena and I have spent so many hours on watching box sets and reality shows. I look at the black shelves next to the couch, which seem so empty now, almost ominous in the half-light, my romance novels and thrillers donated to the charity shop. My eyes alight on the middle shelf, which is no longer empty; someone must have dumped something on it. I dance closer, smiling as I pass a friend from the gym. I tilt my head and narrow my eyes to get a better view; I've definitely drunk too much. It's a vase, a tall, slender black glass vase I've never seen before. Inside it are three black roses, almost elegant with their long-thorned stems and inky petals – except I know the terrifying meaning behind them. The music stops momentarily as the track changes, and I let out a scream.

The room swirls and the edges of my vision are blackening, as dark as the roses that loom in front of me. I place my hand on the wall and breathe deeply, trying to regain my balance.

'Ava, what's the matter?' Steph is wide-eyed, looking around to see what can possibly have upset me. I reach over and switch the music off. The silence is abrupt, like a shot in the dark.

'Who put that there?' I point a shaking finger at the vase. Steph goes to the bookcase and lifts it down.

'Are you talking about this?' She looks perplexed, her eyes moving from me to the other people in the room, who are looking on, puzzled and curious.

The floor is holding my attention now; I can't bear to look at the vase any more. I'm frozen, unable to speak. I shake my head.

'Who brought these flowers?' Steph asks.

Nobody steps forward, like I knew they wouldn't. Everyone is a potential suspect.

'Please, this is important,' I say in a wobbly voice. Gareth walks in from the kitchen. 'Gareth, did you put those roses there?'

He sees everyone staring and clutches the bottle in his hand tighter. 'Of course not. Where's Lena? I already told her I found that rose outside. I wish I hadn't bothered now.' He looks genuinely bewildered, and I'm sure he's telling the truth.

'Did anybody see who brought these roses? They weren't there when the party started.' I look around and take in the bemused expressions of these people – my friends – everyone looking at me as if I'm a crazy woman ranting in the street. 'Please,' I'm sobbing now, my words coming out in a gulp, 'who is sending these? Why won't you stop, why won't you leave me alone?'

Steph thuds the vase down on the table and droplets of inky water rain down on the floor. Lena appears in the doorway.

'What's happened to the music?' She stops when she sees me, looks at the roses. 'I've got this,' she says. 'Put the tunes back on, it's nothing to worry about.'

The music starts again and conversations pick up. Lena puts her arms around me and I sob into her chest. 'Why are you so upset?' she asks.

'Those roses, they weren't here earlier, I know they weren't. I cleared everything off those shelves.' Lena's arms stiffen, then hold me tighter.

'You see now, don't you?' she says. 'The person who put that vase there is at the party. But nobody in here knows what's going on.' She moves her hand from my back to indicate the rest of the room, who are mostly now having earnest conversations and casting curious glances my way.

'Why are the roses bothering you so much, Ava?' Steph asks. 'I don't understand.'

I feel as if my head is going to burst. All these people are here for me, but the only person I want to see is Ben. Why has he still not arrived? My stomach clenches at the thought that something terrible might have happened to him. Whoever is doing this is trying to hurt me; what better way to do that than by harming Ben?

Thoughts race through my mind, so many questions. Is Gareth telling the truth? Could it be Martha? Can I trust anyone? The roses have been sticking their thorns into me for thirteen years. And now, for the first time, their sender is right here.

CHAPTER 31

Lena

I lead Ava out of the living room, leaving Steph behind. The kitchen is empty save for a couple of women, who go back next door when they see us, talking in low voices and looking concerned. We sit down and I smooth Ava's hair out of her eyes. She takes a tissue from the box we keep on the table and wipes her mascara-streaked face.

'We have to find out who is doing this to you,' I say, 'and why. But you know what I think.'

Her hands tremble and she hesitates before the words rush out. 'When I saw that vase, I just lost my mind. It wasn't there earlier, was it? I remember you saying how empty the room felt this afternoon, and I had a good look around as I was feeling nostalgic – that's why I can remember the empty shelves. I was even reminiscing about the day you put them up. I'm gutted to leave, Lena, you must understand that. We've had a great time in this house.'

It's the roses that are driving her away, I think, forcing her to leave. Does she really want to get married, or is it simply a means of escape? When I manage to prove to her who is doing this, she'll want to stay, she will. She needs me.

'My make-up has run,' she says. 'I must look a right state. It's a good job Ben isn't here.' Her smile is unconvincing. 'Maybe you were right when you said that something's up with him. I'm worried now, with all these weird things that are happening. What if he's been hurt – deliberately – and that's why he isn't here?'

'No, I shouldn't have said anything. I'm sorry, I was just frustrated. You mustn't worry.'

'I'm scared to trust anyone. I think I believe Gareth, don't you?'

'I do. He's odd, I know, but … There is one other suspect,' I say.

Our eyes meet.

'You mean Martha.'

I nod. 'It makes sense. Why is she here? I don't trust her. Have you asked her about the other roses?'

'Yes. She didn't know what I was talking about. I believed her, I think.' She chews on her lip. 'She said she wanted to sort things out with me before I go away.'

'But why now?'

'Mum persuaded her.'

'She's trying to turn you against me, that's what her real purpose is.'

'But why would she do that when I'm about to move abroad? It doesn't make sense.'

'Because she thinks I've taken her place and it's gone on for long enough.'

'She hates us being close, she told me that. But there's room for both of you, can't you see?'

'I don't trust her and you shouldn't either. Look, I didn't want to tell you this because it will worry you, but I have to now. Someone threw my framed newspaper article into the fire. Felix found the frame, and when I checked in my room, it had gone. It looks like someone is out to get us both. And you know who was making fun of that article being up on my wall earlier? Martha, that's who. You need to be careful—'

'Why does she need to be careful?' a cut-glass voice interrupts us. We both spin around. My heart thumps against my chest.

Martha leans nonchalantly against the wall, her make-up still immaculate, poised as if she's going off for a television shoot. I stand up.

'You planted the vase of black roses there, didn't you? It's you who's been sending them to Ava. That's why you're back, admit it.'

'Black roses? What vase? I don't know what you're talking about.'

'Yeah, right.' Of course she's denying it. 'They weren't there when the party started. Now you're here, and the roses appear. In a vase that doesn't even belong to this house.'

'I've already discussed this with Ava. What you're saying is ridiculous. I'm just one of loads of other people here. And so what if someone has odd taste in flowers? It was meant to be a gift, surely?'

I'm about to reply when a flash of pink colours the scene, and Lorraine, Ava's running buddy from down the road, appears at Martha's side. In her skin-tight denim jeggings and neon-pink vest top that shows off her muscled arms, she looks tiny compared to Martha.

'I've just realised who you are,' she says. 'Honestly, I've been racking my brain ever since I first saw you this evening, and it's finally come to me.' She giggles, letting out a girlish tinkle. 'It was only when Donna was talking about television chat shows that I realised. You're Martha Thomas, of course; you interviewed that comedian last week and it was a hoot. And you're Ava's sister. How did I not know that, Ava? You kept it very quiet!' Her ponytail bounces up and down as she talks. 'What's it like being on television? I'm a huge fan of yours.'

While she's babbling, the thumping in my chest eases up and I make the most of the distraction by steering Ava away from the pair.

'I understand now,' I say. 'It's the roses; that's why you're leaving, isn't it?' Her eyes fill with tears and I feel a warm rush of hope coursing through my veins. If I can only keep her away from Martha for the rest of the evening, we might be OK. Putting a whole ocean between her and her problems doesn't necessarily mean they will go away, and I have to make her see that.

We hear Felix shouting, 'Ten minutes to midnight, folks, firework time, and then grub's up. Can you all stop your scintillating conversations and come outside? And take a sparkler on your way.' He thrusts a huge box at me and I'm not quick enough to refuse. 'The lovely Lena will hand them out to you.'

'But …'

The corner of the box digs into my ribs, and everyone starts to move towards me, crowding me in a rush of heat.

'Are you OK?' I mouth to Ava, and she nods.

'I'll tell everyone next door,' she says, wiping her eyes, and she's gone before I can stop her.

Hands reach towards me and I plaster a smile on my face as Ava moves out of sight, followed by Martha. It's impossible to keep her in my view, and I pass out sparklers robotically, as if I'm on a factory conveyor belt.

'Shall I do an announcement,' Felix says, 'asking everyone to go into the living room at the end of the fireworks for you know what?' He taps the side of his nose.

'Yes. I haven't had a chance to ask Ava yet, but I'm sure she'll be all right with it.'

'I think Steph sounded her out – without giving anything away, of course – and she reckons it will be fine. It's all going great, isn't it? Everyone outside for fireworks!' he yells, his words followed by a loud bang. 'Whoops.'

He pushes past people back out to the bonfire, where a piece of wood has collapsed, causing the flames to bend towards the house and throwing out a whoosh of heat.

'Everything is under control, folks.'

I wish I could share his assurance.

'I'll have a sparkler if you're offering.' Pete appears in front of me.

'What were you and Kate talking about out there?' I ask, handing him one. The plastic packaging glints in the light; Ava would hate the wastage. The thought annoys me – I have to forget about what she wants.

'Ava, actually. I'd like to apologise to her.'

'Haven't you two had a chance to speak yet?'

'No, Steph interrupted us.'

'Any sparklers left?' a woman asks, and I shove one roughly into her hand, annoyed that Steph seems to be everywhere tonight. The woman rubs her palm as she goes out into the garden, and I dump the empty box on the window ledge.

'Ava doesn't want to talk to you,' I say.

'That's not what Kate said.'

'Kate? She doesn't even know her.'

'That's what you reckon. I don't think you know Ava as well as you make out.' He disappears into the garden as a firework erupts, a flash of green blinding me.

CHAPTER 32

2005

The kitchen was a mess. Empty glasses and crushed cans littered the table along with half-eaten plates of food. Lena hadn't eaten anything. She was more interested in the alcohol. She needed something strong, but the punch bowl was empty. She opened the kitchen cupboards one by one. Up high, hidden at the back, she found a bottle of rum. She'd never tried rum before. She gagged on the first sip but enjoyed the second, the liquid warming her insides, making her feel brave enough to go back into the other room. In the hallway, Ava's sister's friend Tess was putting her coat on, taking a bunch of keys out of her pocket.

'You leaving?' Lena asked.

'Yeah,' Tess said.

'Which way are you going?'

'Back into town. Do you need a lift?'

'That would be great. Let me get Ava. We're stopping over at mine.'

In the lounge, Ava was no longer draped over Danny. She had her back to Lena and turned unsteadily when Lena tapped her on the shoulder. 'We should go. I've sorted out a lift for us.'

'But I don't want to leave.' Ava's eyes looked unfocused.

Danny was listening to their conversation, looking away when Lena caught his eye. Lena gripped Ava's arm, squeezing tight.

'Ouch,' Ava said, shaking her off.

'You're making a show of yourself,' Lena said. She slung her arm around Ava, leading her towards the door. 'Why are you with Danny?'

'We were dancing. I didn't mean anything by it,' Ava replied, her words slurred.

'I want to go now. Are you coming? Tess is going to drop us home.'

Ava pulled a face.

'You're staying at mine, remember. You're out of it, Ava, you need me with you. You're on your own if you stay here. Your parents will find out if you go home. Don't make this difficult.'

'You're right,' Ava said. 'Don't hate me.'

Lena could forgive her friend. She couldn't handle her drink; most likely she wouldn't remember a thing the next day. They were sisters and nothing was going to get in the way of that.

CHAPTER 33

Ava

A shout comes from the garden. 'Last call for fireworks!'

Martha steers me past Lena, who is handing out the last few sparklers with a grimace on her face as if they are hand grenades.

Martha opens the fridge and pulls out the bottle of champagne. 'It's the perfect moment to drink this now,' she says, brandishing it at me. She makes a performance of opening it with a satisfying pop. 'Cheers,' she says as we tap our plastic cups together. Our eyes meet and I bat away that sliver of uncertainty about her that wriggles inside me like a tapeworm.

We head outside, where almost everyone is gathered. Felix is at the far end of the garden, organising the fireworks and indicating how far back people should stand, while Steph hands out baked potatoes blackened in foil. The burnt smell of the crispy skins elicits a burst of hunger in me.

Martha stands to the side of the crowd, arms folded, watching Lena. Should I trust her? I'm flooded with emotion, seeing Martha through my six-year-old eyes, my tall, confident, beautiful sister, who I'd have followed to the ends of the earth. A Catherine wheel spins around, and people gasp and exclaim as they watch the spiralling firework, coloured sparks flying in all directions.

When did I stop trusting my sister? The sparks mirror my emotions, darting here and there. The unconditional love never went away, but everything changed when my parents took Lena in. Martha left home and left me, driven by her antipathy towards Lena. Her judgement was so clouded by everything that had happened, it was impossible to get through to her. In the end, I'd had to make a choice between them, even though I hated it. And Lena was always there, with her devotion and the sacrifice she'd made for me, altering the course of my life – saving me.

That was when I stopped playing the piano. The ability to play just vanished. I'd sit at the keyboard, willing my fingers to work, but each time I moved my left hand, the stitches in the gash in my shoulder would stretch and burn. At first I thought it was entirely down to my injuries, but as they eventually healed, leaving only the scar, and my strength returned, still my fingers refused to play the notes. Deep down, I didn't believe I deserved to play any more. The piano had always soothed me, given me space to mull over my feelings as my fingers ran over the keys. Why would I want time to think ever again? I needed to forget.

Watching the flames as the past flickers along in my mind, I see how Martha was grieving, latching onto her resentment at Lena. She had lost her best friend and then she lost me, and she blamed Lena for that. If we're to trust one another again, she has to let go of that resentment; they both do. I want them both in my life more than anything. And I'm playing my piano again, something I never thought possible.

Martha looks back at me as if she senses me thinking about her, then walks swiftly over, taking my arm.

'Come with me,' she says. 'Now's our chance.'

'What are we doing?' I ask, but even after all these years, it's second nature for me to follow my big sister. I'm six again, trailing her everywhere, my little feet tripping over themselves in their urge to keep up with her longer strides, letting her decide what games we're to play that day. We go upstairs through the house, which is quiet now the music has been turned down, and she stops outside Lena's room.

'What are you doing?'

'When do you remember last having your phone?' she asks.

'In here.' I indicate Lena's room. 'When we were getting ready. I kept checking for a message from Ben. I had a quick look earlier, but I couldn't see it.'

'I'm convinced it must be in here. Lena's busy outside; it's the ideal moment.'

Even though I wouldn't normally think twice about going into Lena's room, with Martha in tow it feels wrong. I see through my sister's eyes the chaos of make-up and clothes, the mess of Lena's life. My desire for harmony between them seems unachievable at this point in time, with so much happening that I don't understand.

'I thought she was supposed to be moving out tomorrow?' Martha says, going over to the bed and looking around. 'She obviously hasn't made any effort. Still, Mum said she knows the owner, so maybe she can decide to stay longer.' She shrugs. 'I never did understand that girl. I guess some things don't change.'

I leave the door open, feeling guilty to be here. But my sister has no such qualms, pulling open the wardrobe door and rooting through Lena's clothes, feeling in pockets.

'What are you doing Martha?'

'I'm looking to see where that bitch—'

'Don't call her a bitch,' I say.

'Fine. I'm looking to see where your *friend* has hidden your mobile.'

I set down the pile of books I've just picked up to check that my phone hasn't fallen behind them, stunned.

'Deliberately, you mean? Why would she do that?'

She shrugs. 'Let's see if we can find it first, then I'll explain what I mean. I'm hoping I'm wrong.'

'You know, the roses aren't the only thing that's happened to me recently. Somebody has scratched my face out in all my photographs.'

'You're serious?'

'I had some old photograph albums out and I couldn't help flicking through them. In every photo in which I appeared, my face had been scrubbed out. Only mine, the others were all left intact. Somebody hates me that much.'

'That's awful. That's why this is important. If we find nothing, we can rule Lena out.'

'But what could Lena possibly have to do with any of this?'

Martha ignores me, going through Lena's drawers. I cringe as she rifles through her underwear, lifting out her padded bras and lacy knickers. Finally she lets out a long breath.

'Nothing,' she says. 'I was convinced we'd find something. What's this all about?'

'Tell me what you meant just now.'

She hesitates. 'I think there's something going on between her and Ben.'

I drop down onto the bed, winded. 'How can you say that? They don't even like each other.'

'Think about it. It doesn't make sense that he wouldn't be in touch, and she's being so secretive about his whereabouts. So what if it's a surprise party; he'd know not to say anything to you if he spoke to you. He's not a child, is he?'

'But she barely knows him; it doesn't make sense. And he wants me away from Lena, he's made that clear.'

'Exactly – maybe he wants you away from her because something has gone on between them.'

I shake my head, refusing to believe it. 'No way, she—'

But Martha is distracted, peering at the top of the wardrobe. 'Hang on, there's something up there.' Standing on tiptoes, she pulls down a shoebox. Dust flies into the air. She holds the box against her chest, opens it and lets out a whistle.

'What is it?' Nothing can be worse than my obliterated face in the photographs. Or could it?

'Unbelievable,' Martha says. 'What is she up to?'

She takes something out of the box and turns to face me, brandishing it in her hand. It's my passport.

CHAPTER 34
Lena

Fizzing sparklers are held in the air as Felix lets off the fireworks, which whoosh up through the air, exploding in showers of multicoloured sparks. The fire crackles and the smell of the bonfire fills my nose and throat, making me cough as I look around for Ava. Where is she? I'm sure I saw her come out. She should be here for the celebration. This is all for her. As I scan the crowd, with my heart in my smoke-filled throat, it dawns on me that she's not here, and Martha's nowhere to be seen either.

I look over to the house, but the kitchen is empty, glasses and plates abandoned on the table. I peer towards the far end of the garden, where Felix is managing the firework display, helped by Steph, everyone else kept back at a suitable distance. Then a figure with dark hair bobs into my vision. It's Kate, and I'm sure she's rummaging around in the stash of fireworks behind the tree. What is she doing? I still don't know what she wanted to ask me, and my stomach feels jumpy at the thought. I make my way down towards the bonfire, studying the faces as I go in case I've missed Ava, but my churning gut tells me she's not out here. She must be inside with Martha. I hope she'll challenge her about the roses again. That woman gets away with too much, always has done.

'Keep back,' Felix says. 'Oh, it's you, Lena.' Black streaks mark his face, but his eyes are shining with excitement. 'Isn't this great?'

A firework whistles past us up into the sky, erupting in an explosion of green and yellow. 'Look at that.' He shakes his head. 'Awesome.'

'What is she doing?' I ask, indicating Kate.

Steph and Felix look where I'm pointing.

'Oh, it's OK, Kate's been helping us,' Steph says. 'Felix has told her what order he wants everything in.' She rolls her eyes. 'He's got a spreadsheet. I told you he was taking this seriously.'

'Do you know Kate?' I ask.

Steph shrugs. 'Not prior to this evening, but she's going out with the guy from Accounts and that's good enough for me. Why?'

I shrug. 'Just wondered. She seems to know Pete as well.'

'Really?' Steph says. 'I think Pete might have left. I haven't seen him for ages.'

A series of bangs makes me jump as a rush of fireworks shoot into the air, one after the other, bursting into a shower of colours. I look up at my bedroom window. The blind is down, but light peeps through the slats. I swear I see movement behind it, but it's hard to be sure. Still no sign of Martha or Ava. Instincts prickling, I make my way over to Kate.

'What are you doing?'

'Calm down, Lena. I'm making myself useful, sorting these into order for Felix. He's very specific, isn't he? Or anal, whichever you prefer. Here you are, Felix,' she says, handing him what looks like a rocket, flashing him a huge smile as she does. Everyone is laughing and whooping as each new firework flies into the sky, making exaggerated oohs and aahs with every explosion. I wish I could join in the merriment, but there are too many things bothering me. Including Kate.

'Ava says you wanted to talk to me about something.'

'Oh yes. This house, it's fabulous. In a great area. She said you could have extended the contract if you'd wanted. I'd be interested in moving in.'

'Don't be ridiculous.' An explosion above us has me jumping again, Kate's recklessness making me feel even more on edge.

'Thanks, Kate,' Felix says. 'I've got the next ten minutes sorted and that should pretty much be it.'

'No worries,' Kate says, and sits down on the ground, picking up a bottle of beer from beside her. 'I've been saving this. Now my work is done.' She looks at me, her face hard. 'For the moment, that is. Stay and have a drink with me.' She produces another beer, takes a bottle opener from her back pocket and flips the lid off.

I hesitate, checking once more for Ava before sitting down next to Kate.

'You shouldn't have come. I told you I'd deal with this,' I say.

'Well she's still going, isn't she, jetting off to New York to be with lover boy. Swanning around tonight in her designer dress as if she hasn't a care in the world.'

'Hardly. She's lost her phone and her passport, and she's stressing about lover boy not turning up.'

'And will he?'

'Apparently he's been delayed.' I take a sip of beer, running my tongue around my lips. 'I told you I'd sort it. I still think you should go, it's too risky.'

'I see her sister's here,' Kate says, ignoring me. I know what she's doing, flirting with danger. 'Martha Thomas.' She rolls the words around her tongue as if trying them out for size. 'Of course I've got nothing against her. It's Ava who's responsible.'

'Leave it, Kate, we agreed.'

'Right, folks, time for the big one now,' Felix says in a loud voice that carries across the garden. 'And then after that I'd like everyone to gather in the living room, where we'll be saying our goodbyes to Ava. Rumour has it something special has been planned, so you won't want to be ordering your cabs yet. OK. Is everybody ready?'

A huge cheer goes up. Time to find Ava and bring her downstairs for the final surprise. I scramble to my feet.

'Better get out of the way, you two.' Felix nods at us and we both step away. A light at the top of the house catches my eye, and I notice that the blind in my room is moving. The slats inch up and an unmistakable profile appears in the window. Martha. What the hell is she doing in my room?

She looks down over the garden in her imperious way, like a queen surveying her underlings, and our eyes meet. At my side, Kate looks up at her too. Then a whistle, a roar and a mighty bang make my hands fly to my ears as the rocket launches into the air in a blaze of purple and silver sparks, leaving a shiny tail of smoke and a whistling sound vibrating in my head. When I look back at the window, the blind is down again and my room is in darkness. And Kate is no longer beside me.

CHAPTER 35
2005

Ava rubbed her arm where Lena had pinched her, while Lena went to fetch their coats from upstairs. She didn't want to leave the party. The drink was making her head spin, but in a good way, and dancing with Danny had made her glow inside and out. She felt a stab of guilt as she caught sight of him and saw the way he was looking at her. Lena liked him too, but they were best friends and no way would they fall out over a boy. Friendship was way more important, wasn't it? But the guilt was followed by a rush of pleasure.

He was back at her side as soon as Lena had gone. 'What did she want?' he asked.

'We have to go.'

'Why? It's only just gone midnight.'

'Yeah, but I'm staying with Lena and she wants to leave.'

'What's up with your arm?'

Ava was still rubbing the red blemish where Lena's fingers had twisted her skin.

'Lena. She didn't mean it. She's kind of forceful sometimes – but not in a bad way or anything.'

'I bet she is. She was after me earlier, but I'm not interested. I'm only interested in one girl here.' His brown eyes were looking directly at Ava, causing her stomach to flutter. His gaze dropped to her mouth, and it felt natural when his lips touched hers. His hands roamed over her back, his touch cold but welcome against her warm skin.

'You're beautiful,' he said, looking deep into her eyes.

'So are you,' she said, but the ceiling was rotating and she gasped when a hand gripped her shoulder.

CHAPTER 36

Ava

Martha waves the passport at me. Behind her, the sky explodes with colour and the gold lettering on the passport glints.

'What is she doing with your passport hidden in her room?' She peers out into the garden. Lena is staring up in our direction. 'Look at her, giving me the evil eye. I wouldn't put it past her to blast a rocket at me, obliterate me once and for all.'

'Martha, don't be silly. She can't even see you from down there.'

'Not literally, obviously. Who's that with her?' She moves closer to the window, narrowing her eyes, but as I step forward, a loud bang makes me jump, and by the time I've refocused my eyes, Lena has disappeared, as has whoever was with her. The constant explosions from outside haven't helped my shattered nerves, and I sit down on the bed, only now hit by the reality of what Lena having my passport means. She's actively trying to stop me going. How could she? But no, she wouldn't do that. Has Martha somehow engineered this? I shake my head. Crazy ideas, I'm going crazy. A thought darts into my head and my heart beats even faster.

'I hope my ticket is still in my case.' My heart is thumping against my chest more loudly than the fireworks rocketing outside.

'How did you book it?'

'On my phone. Should I go and have another look?'

'No, you're getting yourself wound up. Try and stay calm. Even if she's taken that too you've got a record of it and you'll be able to use the mobile ticket, or reprint it.' The panic recedes a little and I can breathe again. 'Keep this somewhere safe.' She hands me the passport.

My fingertips are white as I clutch it to me. I thought my suitcase was safe, my room a sanctuary at this party with my friends, people who supposedly care for me. But I don't know who to trust any more. Looking over the garden at the guests outside, the smoky faces are blurred, just like my emotions. I'm not even sure about my own sister; what do I know of her over the past few years, what resentments have been building? Is she really on my side? Blood must count for something. I want to trust her, but the most important thing is keeping myself safe. And that means trusting nobody.

'I can't leave it in my room again,' I say, 'but I haven't got a bag.'

'Let me look after it.'

I hesitate, and she purses her lips.

'Seriously? I was the one who found it, remember. I'll keep it safe for you, I promise.'

'Of course.' I hand it over, hoping she doesn't feel the trembling in my fingers. The passport is just one part of the equation. So many pieces need resolving before my way forward becomes clear.

Martha paces round in slow circles. Her movements are so familiar from when we were growing up, and I wish it was just the logistics of a game of hide-and-seek she was organising now. Dread is creeping through me, darting through each vein, as realisation dawns. Ben and Lena. It would explain why she would do this. An affair. My passport. 'We've got Lena all wrong.' My voice sounds strangely calm, even as my world is shattering like the fireworks in the garden, which are relentless now. 'She doesn't want to keep me here; she wants to take my place.'

Martha nods. 'No wonder she reacted badly when you mentioned the engagement. If Ben hasn't told her, she'll be furious. She won't know how far she can trust him. Come on, let's go; we don't want her to know we've been in here.'

Another firework bangs and a thought hits me. The ring. I can't get across the landing to my own room quickly enough.

'Oh no, oh my God, my engagement ring, what if she's taken that too?' I drop to my knees and rummage in my case, no longer bothered about keeping the clothes neatly folded. I grab hold of the scarf and my heart thuds as the ring box drops to the floor. My fingers fumble as I try and open it as fast as I can. Martha takes it from me gently and I hold my breath.

'Wow,' she says, seeing the huge diamond sparkling in the dim light of the room. 'It's a beauty.'

'Thank God.' I exhale with relief. 'For a moment there I was convinced she'd taken that too. Can you imagine?' I stroke the diamond before slipping the ring onto my engagement finger. 'There's only one way to keep this safe.' The ring feels strange on my hand, a heavy presence. I swivel it so that the diamond is facing my palm. 'I still think she's trying to take my place, though,' I say.

'Well I'm here and I won't let that happen. Even if she is having an affair with Ben, would he really want to give up the relationship the two of you have built up over several years? Those are conversations that will need to be had. For now, our main priority is finding out exactly what she's up to. Don't say anything about the passport ...' She strokes my arm as I go to protest. 'I know it's hard, but this way we're one step ahead of her. You need to tell me everything, though. What was all that about downstairs earlier? Why were you so upset about the roses? You didn't explain it properly.'

I take a deep breath. 'I was dancing when I noticed a vase of black roses in the living room. Someone has been tormenting me with them ever since the accident. One a year. On the anniversary. Until today. It's as if they're trying to warn me. The roses weren't there when the party started. Then you arrived, and they appeared. That's what Lena meant. I thought it might be Gareth, because he turned up with one. Or you.'

'Me?' Martha looks incredulous. 'I'm your sister. Whatever happens, I would never hurt you. And I can't believe it of Gareth either; it doesn't strike me as the kind of thing he'd do. It's not his style. It's too calculated, too organised. The Gareth I used to know stumbled from one day to the next. I can't imagine him changing that much.'

'You're right, but Lena said—'

'I wouldn't listen to anything Lena tells you,' Martha says. 'That woman has serious problems. You're better off without her.'

'I can't stop thinking about it,' I say. Horrible images tumble around my head. 'What if she's planning on going to New York in my place?' Lena wouldn't do that, would she? She's meant to be my sister.

'Stop torturing yourself. What we need to do is talk to Ben.'

'Has Mum got back to you yet?'

'No, but there are other ways. I could contact him via Facebook.'

'He doesn't use it. He deliberately stays away from social media, says it distracts him from his work too much. The only one he uses is LinkedIn. Can you contact people on that?'

'Not sure, but I doubt it. I could try.' Martha takes her phone out of her pocket and taps and scrolls until she finds what she wants.

'There he is. Benjamin James.'

The photo he uses is one I took on my first trip to the States. He was smiling at me, and his expression is open, friendly, dark hair flopping in front of one eye. Not the sort of man who would go behind my back with my best friend, surely? I've always trusted him, but with the huge distance between us, I realise there is so much I don't know, so many opportunities for the strength of our relationship to be tested. His strange mood last time flashes into my head again.

'I've sent him a message,' Martha says. 'Do you want to go back downstairs?'

'What time is it?' I ask.

'Twelve thirty.'

'I don't have much choice. Most people are still here. And I need to have it out with Lena, find out exactly what's going on.'

'I'll stay with you, we'll do this together. But hold back what we know so far; see what she says.' She slings her arm around me. 'I won't let her hurt you, don't worry. Let's watch the rest of the fireworks before we go down.'

We stand close to the window, Martha's arm warm against my back. Outside, Felix steps onto an old crate and addresses everyone.

'Right, folks, time for the big one now,' Felix says in a booming voice that echoes in the air. 'And then after that I'd like everyone to gather in the living room, where we'll be saying our goodbyes to Ava. Rumour has it something special has been planned, so you won't want to be ordering your cabs yet. OK. Is everybody ready?'

Martha raises her eyebrows as a loud cheer goes up.

'Do you know what's happening next?' she asks.

'I'm not entirely certain. Steph mentioned my piano, and I've been working on a piece of music, but I'm not sure I want to know exactly what she's got planned. Nerves will only go and spoil it.'

A huge bang fills the room and the sound of a rocket shooting off whistles in my ears. Purple and silver sparks tumble through the air. A split second of eerie silence is followed by a burst of applause and cheers. Watching the explosion of colour and the reactions of my friends fills me with warmth, despite everything.

'Hey, listen,' Martha says, nudging me in the ribs. 'Can you hear that?'

A chant rises into the air where moments ago smoke and colour filled the sky.

'Ava, Ava, Ava.'

She squeezes my waist, then slips her arm through mine. 'Sounds like your public awaits you. We'd better give them what they want.'

CHAPTER 37

2005

Lena stomped up the stairs thinking about Danny. He hadn't paid Lena any attention all evening. She wanted him to notice her. She'd bought the push-up bra especially. She pictured Ava dancing with him and she wanted to scream.

The music had slowed down and the thumping beat from downstairs made the floor shake. She could feel the cider she'd shared with an incredibly tall boy in the kitchen sloshing around in her stomach. She belched and cursed as a heap of coats slid from the bed onto her feet, and she kicked them around with her shoe, holding onto the door frame to stop the room from swirling around.

Eventually she untangled Ava's jacket. Her own borrowed fur one was underneath, and she pulled it on, stopping momentarily when a waft of perfume overwhelmed her. She stuck her nose into the collar of Ava's jacket and inhaled a mixture of lemon shampoo and floral fragrance. It should be sickly, but nothing about Ava could ever be sickly. A sense of Ava overpowered her. She wanted her; not *her* exactly, but everything she had – her expensive perfume, her family, her life. And Danny.

She told herself they were only dancing. Ava was her soulmate, her sister, and she was a good person; she wouldn't do that to her. She ran downstairs, her mood lifted, and stopped in the living room doorway looking for her friend. Ava was facing Danny, close to him, too close, gazing into those chocolate-brown eyes that Lena thought about in bed at night. Lena was unable to move as she watched Ava stretch her body upwards, her lips reaching for Danny's, her arms sliding around his back. Something snapped in her, and she hurtled across the room and slammed her hand down on Ava's shoulder.

CHAPTER 38
Lena

The blast from the final firework is ringing in my ears and flashes of purple and silver flicker in and out of my sight as the crowd chants Ava's name. Felix mouths 'Get Ava' at me and I nod, not needing any encouragement to hurry inside. A man sitting on the sofa raises his glass at me as I go through the lounge, a sloppy smile on his face.

Ava and Martha are coming down the stairs. Challenging Martha about being in my room will have to wait. I don't want anything to spoil this for Ava; it has to go perfectly. 'What's going on, Lena? We heard Felix's announcement,' Martha says.

I address Ava. 'Come with me. Everyone wants to give you a proper send-off. Don't look so alarmed.' I smile at her and take her elbow, leading her into the lounge, which is now full of people. She is rubbing the scar on her shoulder and I gently remove her hand like I've seen Sue do so many times. She gives me a rueful smile.

'How could you do this to me?' But her eyes shine, and I cling to the belief that deep down she knows she can trust me.

'Hooray!' everyone yells, clapping.

Ava smiles, hesitant at first, then her mouth widens as she sees her friends gathered for her and I know I've done the right thing. No matter what other random stuff has been going on this evening, this is for her. Her special moment. She fusses with her hair and clears her throat.

'Thanks, guys,' she says. Somebody whoops and everybody laughs.

'Speech,' yells a voice, and a glass of something fizzy is shoved into her hand. Surely she won't mention the wedding, as Ben isn't here. Everyone knowing would make it more final.

'There's no need for all this fuss,' she says. 'All I want to do is thank you for coming, and I hope everyone is having a great time.'

'Yay,' says Steph, followed by various noises of approval from the crowd.

'Of course I have to thank Felix for organising such a brilliant firework display. If you didn't know it already, he's a fireman, so I had no worries that you were in any danger whatsoever.'

Felix raises his tweed cap at Ava and gives a mock bow.

'I'm also really happy that my sister Martha is here. As some of you may know, it's been a while.' Martha stands in the doorway with a smug smile on her face, and Lorraine beams at her, clapping, her neon-pink top shimmering in the light. I don't even pretend to smile; all I can see is Martha's face staring down at me from my bedroom window. As soon as this is over, I want to know exactly what she was up to. And there's still no sign of Kate.

Ava continues. 'I was hoping that Ben, my fiancé …' she stresses the word, and everybody starts wolf-whistling and clapping, 'would be here.' She looks at me and I can't read her expression, but I don't miss the glint of gold from her finger. 'He hasn't arrived yet, but what does it matter as long as everyone is having a great time.' They all cheer, but Ava gestures for silence. 'Finally, and most importantly of all,' she says, 'I'd like to thank my dear friend Lena, who has organised all this.'

Everyone raises their glasses and Ava taps hers against mine, and as our eyes meet, my chest swells with pride. I don't want this moment to end, but she quickly looks away.

'Three cheers for Ava,' Felix says. 'Hip hip hooray …' As the crowd cheer rowdily, I scan the room. Kate is definitely not here.

Felix holds his hand up.

'Watch out, the fireman wants to make an announcement,' somebody says to calls of 'Fireman Sam!' and 'Where's your uniform?' causing Steph to roll her eyes.

Felix waits for the laughter to stop, clearly enjoying himself.

'Lastly – and I promise I'll shut up after this, but this is something you won't want to miss – as some of you know, Ava is a talented pianist. She was very good when she was young, but life intervened, as the saying goes. Her mother kept her piano, and in the last few months Ava has started playing again. Rumour has it she's written a piece of music. We'd be honoured if you'd play it for us now, Ava.'

A huge cheer goes up and Ava's cheeks and neck flush red. People move aside as she walks over to the piano stool. I follow her and place my hand gently on her back. 'You don't mind, do you?' I whisper in her ear. She shakes her head, and her eyes are shining.

She flexes her fingers over the keys without touching them, as she always does before playing. I love watching her elegant hands floating there, creating the most beautiful sounds with the lightest of touches. She tried to give me lessons back in the day, but my clumsy fingers got in the way.

'OK,' she says, 'I'm ready.'

The room falls quiet. Expectation hovers in the air, and the faces of Ava's friends and colleagues are full of hope and love. It's a shame her parents aren't here to witness this, but people are holding up their phones expectantly, videos set to record, cameras poised to freeze the moment.

Ava squares her shoulders, her back ramrod straight, as upright as the piano itself. She's always held herself like a ballerina, and her shoulders rise as she takes a deep breath. The blue silk of her dress ripples. A pin dropping could be heard in the room as everyone watches in silence. She raises her right hand and presses a key. Nothing happens. She hunches slightly and presses it once more. Still no sound. She pushes her finger down repeatedly on the key, but the only noise it makes is a muffled thud. She holds it down and releases it slowly. Still nothing. Somebody coughs.

'Never mind the fireman, does anyone know a piano tuner?' a voice calls out, and people laugh. Others look embarrassed, willing the piano to respond to Ava's touch. I'm wringing my hands, desperate for this to go right for her. It was working fine last time she played.

She looks at Felix, frowning.

'Technical hitch,' he says. 'Talk amongst yourselves for a moment.' Conversations start, quietly at first and growing louder as Ava gets to her feet.

'Can you lift the top?' she asks Felix, and Gareth jumps forward to help him.

I've seen her look inside the piano many times, finding its mechanism fascinating: the way the little felt-covered hammers hit the strings to make the notes. Now she kneels on the piano stool and strands of her hair fall forward as she leans over to peer in. Her ribs press against the fabric of her dress. Whatever she sees makes her gasp aloud, and she springs back, her hands landing on the left-hand side of the piano, the keys resounding in a deep, jarring sound. I grab her to stop her losing her balance.

Felix and Gareth are still holding the lid up, both trying to see what the problem is. Steph beats them to it and climbs on the stool to look into the dark space. 'What the …' She reaches down, the effort showing on her face as people press forward to see what's going on. 'Ouch!' She pulls her left hand out, and a drop of blood falls onto the keys. She sucks at her finger, then leans in again, stretching down and bringing her hands out, releasing a flurry of dark petals onto the stark white keys. The whole room falls silent.

'What on earth?' Felix looks at her as he and Gareth lower the top back down.

'They're rose petals, it's full of them. Hang on, something weird happened with roses earlier on, didn't it?'

Ava breathes in deeply, and I feel her ribs expand against her back. Murmured conversations have started around us, excited and worried. I snatch a glance at Martha, who has come to Ava's side and is looking sceptical.

'Oh my God,' I say, reaching to touch Ava's arm, 'are you OK?' She shakes my hand away and draws herself up to her full height.

'Felix,' she says, 'help me take these out, and then I'll play. Give me a couple of minutes, everybody,' she says, her voice quiet at first but gaining strength.

Felix holds the piano lid up again while Gareth and Steph scoop out the petals and three thorny rose stems. I can't tell whether these are the same roses that were in the vase on the bookcase earlier. Whether they are or not, it's clear to me now that someone is trying to sabotage the evening. But who, and who exactly are they targeting? It was my frame on the bonfire. Kate appearing – what if someone has sent her? Could they be trying to ruin the party to get at me? Does somebody know the truth?

'They're all out,' Steph says, pressing a tissue against her finger. 'You sure you want to do this, Ava?' She sweeps the petals onto the floor, her lip curled in distaste.

'Oh yes,' Ava says, 'more than anything.'

She sits back down on the piano stool, aligns her posture and tests the notes that previously were stuck. A clear sound rings out.

'Before I start,' she says, 'I have a message for whoever has been trying to upset me this evening.' People exchange worried looks, faces creased with consternation, bewilderment, disbelief. 'Nothing can take away from me what I am about to do.'

She raises and lowers her shoulders, then lifts her hands, the diamond sparkling as if in triumph, and begins playing a beautiful tune to the mesmerised crowd.

When she has finished, she stands and turns to face the room, her friends rushing forward to circle her with their arms. Martha is leaning in the doorway, watching as I scan the crowd, looking for guilty faces.

CHAPTER 39

Ava

While people are still congratulating me on my piano playing, Steph comes over with Mum's cake on a plate, one candle flickering in the middle. Everyone cheers as I blow it out, screwing my eyes shut and wishing for a hitch-free journey to New York.

'Help yourself to cake,' Steph tells them.

'And thanks again for coming,' I add.

Bob Marley's 'Jamming' bursts into the room, and some people start dancing. It's a favourite of mine ordinarily, but now the happy music feels out of place, the elation I felt immediately after playing gone. Was it enough to exorcise those demons? The last time I was scheduled to play was the service one year after the accident, in memory of Tess, at school. The feeling of all those eyes watching me, drilling their accusations into my head, didn't leave me afterwards. I closed the piano lid and walked off stage and didn't play again until recently. He's never even heard me play.

Ben. What has happened to him? It would have been so perfect for him to be here when I announced our engagement. But this party is anything but perfect.

Some guests are leaving now, and I force a smile, try and look as if I'm having the best time. The acrid smell of bonfire still wafts from people's clothes. Martha takes my elbow.

'You played beautifully. I'm so proud of you for not letting the roses put you off. I'm convinced this is down to Lena.'

'But she was there, comforting me. She wouldn't do this. Although she did say she sensed Ben was reluctant to come.' I tell Martha exactly what Lena told me earlier.

'I think we should have it out with her. Let's go and speak to her now. Don't give too much away; be subtle. And don't mention the passport. What we want is for her to trip herself up. She'll deny everything, of course, and we need to catch her out.'

Friends flash smiles at me as I follow Martha through to the kitchen on unsteady feet, and I smile back, the expression feeling unnatural as worry churns inside me. A woman stands in the kitchen eating a slice of cake. She raises her eyebrows at me, making an apologetic face.

'Yum,' she says when she's swallowed her mouthful, licking icing from her fingers. 'That is one delicious cake. Who made it?'

'My mother.'

'She has to be a professional, right?' She sets her plate down on the table, next to what remains of the cake. But this one is made of plain sponge with dark red jam inside and black icing. Mum always makes me chocolate cake, my favourite. 'I'll cut you a piece if you like,' she says.

'No thanks.' My voice sounds strangled. This isn't my mum's cake. This is the cake I shoved out of sight and tried to push out of my mind. The cake that was delivered with no note on, sender unknown. The number 13 has been sliced in two, and only the half with the 1 on remains.

Martha notices that the colour has drained from my face. 'What's up?' she asks.

'This cake turned up earlier and we don't know who sent it. It had the number thirteen on it.'

'Thirteen meaning …?'

I pull a face. 'Lena and I assumed it's to signify thirteen years since …'

'Oh.' Her eyes flash with sadness and she pushes her hair out of her face, looking less composed. 'This is all getting a bit weird.'

'What I want to know is who got it out of the fridge, and why.'

Martha turns to the woman. 'Did you see who cut this cake?'

'No, a couple of people were handing it out. A guy gave me mine; battered leather jacket, bit scruffy-looking.'

'Some people never change,' Martha says. 'Sounds suspiciously like Gareth to me. But anybody could have wandered in here after a few drinks and spotted a cake in the fridge. It's hardly a crime.'

'No, but it could be connected.'

'Wait here,' she says. 'Get yourself a drink. I'll be back in a sec.'

I cut a slice of the cake and put it on a paper napkin. The sponge is light, well baked and looks like a normal Victoria sponge. It smells normal too. My suspicious mind is telling me it could be poisoned, but I shake my head to get rid of the ridiculous thought. It's me who's the target of this vendetta, not my guests.

Martha comes back in followed by Kate, who is holding a tray with a few slices of the cake left on it. Lena trails behind her, going over to the fridge and taking out a bottle of beer.

'Mystery solved,' Martha says. 'Gareth is asleep on the sofa – apparently he's been out of it for ages – but Kate saw who got the cake out of the fridge.'

'It was Pete,' Kate says. 'Hey, Pete!' she calls out into the garden, and I haven't the energy to stop her. 'We didn't know where you guys were, but seeing as half of it had been eaten we thought it had been left for us. Did I do something wrong?'

'No, it's fine,' Martha says. 'We don't know where it came from, that's all.'

Pete appears in the doorway. 'Why are you all looking at me as if I've committed a crime?'

'You took this cake out of the fridge, didn't you?' Kate asks.

'Yes, so what?'

'Why are you still here, Pete?' I tear my eyes away from the cake and look at him properly for the first time. 'Wasn't harassing me at work enough?'

'I apologised to you. I was an idiot; I hate myself for it.'

'The cake?' Kate waves the plate at him.

'It's just a cake. Jesus, can't you all chill out? If you don't want it, I'll chuck it on the fire.'

Lena freezes, bottle of beer held aloft in one hand.

'Why would you say that?' she asks. 'Was it you who threw my picture frame on the fire?'

'What?' I say.

Kate crosses to Pete. 'Come on, mate, time you were getting off, I think.'

Pete holds his hands up. 'I give up. I'll never understand you women.' He follows Kate out of the room.

'For God's sake, Lena,' Martha says. 'Why do you have to make everything about you?'

'Are you sure *you* don't know anything about it, Martha?' Lena is trying to get the lid off her beer bottle. 'It seems to me strange things are happening now you're back.' The cap is tight and her arm tenses as she twists hard. She eventually gets it open just as Kate comes back in.

'Where's Ben, Lena?' Martha asks.

Lena is about to take a drink, but she stops, bottle frozen in front of her.

'Am I psychic?'

Martha rolls her eyes. 'We don't think you're being straight with us about his whereabouts.'

Lena looks from Martha to me, her expression wary. 'Is that what *you* think?' she says, addressing me. 'What is this?'

'Where's your phone?' I ask.

'Seriously? You want to go through my phone? I can't believe you're falling for Martha's game.'

'Let me see it and then I'll apologise. I'm worried, I just want to know where Ben is.'

'I know you don't want to hear this, but maybe it's his way of letting you down gently.'

'You keep saying that and then going back on it. Has he said something to you?'

'Of course not. You wouldn't believe me anyway, the way you're behaving tonight.'

'Oh God,' I say, slumping down onto a chair. 'I'm scared, Lena.'

'Of what?'

I take a deep, unsteady breath. 'I—'

Martha interrupts me. 'Is something going on between you and Ben, Lena? Is that why you're being so cagey? Ava's worried that something has happened to him. Is that what you want?'

Lena laughs out loud. 'Of course not. I hope you aren't listening to her lies, Ava. I'm sorry Ben isn't here yet, but it's not my fault. What I want is for you to enjoy yourself. That's why I organised this party. You must know that.'

'And it's a great party,' Kate says, putting a piece of cake into her mouth. I'd forgotten she was there. Lena glares at her and I don't understand what it means. Maybe she asked Lena about moving in and Lena didn't want to know. She doesn't seem to want to stay in this house at all without me.

'Leave it, will you?' Lena spits the words out, but Kate doesn't look fazed.

'Where is Pete?' I ask.

'He's gone home. I put him in a cab.'

The tension in my shoulders eases a little. One less thing to worry about.

Kate and Lena are still staring at one another. A series of bangs from down the street makes us all jump.

'Great,' Kate says. 'Another display. I wonder if we can see it from your garden.' She wanders outside, glancing at Lena as she goes.

'Listen to me,' Martha says. 'Trashing your room when you find out your supposed best friend is getting married is not a normal reaction. You should be happy for her.' She turns her attention to me. 'She doesn't care about you, Ava, and I'm glad you're getting away. All she cares about is herself. What's going to happen to her when you move to New York? Because she won't be able to cling to you any more, the way she's spent her whole life doing.'

Lena looks at me, and I know what she's thinking before she says it. 'Have you forgotten what happened?'

A gulf of sadness wells up inside me. As if I could ever forget.

'Of course I haven't forgotten,' I tell her. 'You saved my life that day. I owe everything to you. But I understand you now, Martha. Why you had to leave. At the time I was too wrapped up in myself. I resented you for leaving home and not being there for me. I didn't understand why you two couldn't just get on. But I know now that you were grieving and I should have realised that then. Staying at home meant you couldn't get away from it. But Lena was there, she was the one who was there for me and helped me build myself up again. It's thanks to her you've still got a sister.' My voice catches in my throat. I don't want to tell Martha about the day Lena found me slumped in my university room, losing consciousness after all the pills I'd taken. None of my family know about that.

'Don't trust her,' Lena says. 'She's here for a reason. Her intentions are black, like the roses she's been sending.'

Martha laughs. 'How poetic. She's fooling you. That pathetic newspaper article up on her wall. Wallowing in the past, her fifteen-minute claim to fame. I've never believed in those heroics anyway.'

'You weren't there. How can you say that? I saved your sister's life, Martha. What is wrong with you? I know it's you who's been sending the roses.'

'Prove it,' Martha says, her eyes fierce.

'We don't know for sure it wasn't Gareth, unlikely as it is,' I say.

'Martha could have put him up to it. She'd do anything to get at you.'

'Maybe I've made a mistake coming here,' Martha says. 'I wanted to sort things out with you before you go, Ava, but I can't get near you because of her. Which is what made me stay away in the first place. Why can't you see through her? I hope you'll make a clean break when you go.'

'Why can't you two stop fighting? I've had enough.'

'Because I don't trust her and you shouldn't either,' says Lena. 'Has she told you that she's forgiven you? She'll never let you forget what you did to Tess. Because that's what all this is about, isn't it?'

A memory flashes into my head of Tess in the kitchen at that party, the sparkle in her eye when she talked about passing her driving test, twisting the keys in her hands with pride. The scar on my shoulder twinges, and I rub my fingers over it to calm it down. After what I did, I deserve to be here fighting with these women, my best friend and my sister, abandoned by my boyfriend and feeling uncertain about a future that only yesterday I thought I had sorted. I thought I knew Ben, but in one evening my confidence in our relationship has been undone. The scar is throbbing now and I struggle to breathe. I want to get away from this atmosphere, which is cloying like the sickly smell of roses.

Just then Kate comes back into the kitchen. Martha looks at her quizzically.

'Do I know you?' she asks. 'I'm sure I've met you before.'

Kate shakes her head, shrugging into the jacket she's carrying, extracting a car key from her pocket. 'Don't think so.'

'How do you know Ava?'

'I'm a friend of a friend.'

'You mean you don't recognise the great Martha Thomas?' says Lena, her tongue curling around the words in distaste.

Kate's hand pauses in zipping up her jacket.

'I'm a TV presenter,' Martha tells her.

'I don't watch television. Anyway, thanks for the party, guys. Lena, it was great to catch up.'

CHAPTER 40
2005

Ava shrugged the hand off her shoulder. She was aware she was drunk; everything was magnified. Yellow balloons were swirling around the room and everyone was jumping, trying to hit one. A mass of yellow floated towards her like flying blancmange and she broke away from Danny. The party was happening around her, people jostling and bumping into her, dancers knocking against her, music pounding in her head, the room a seething mass.

Bright lights flashed. She was looking for something. She screwed up her forehead in concentration. The insistent beat of the music was pulsing underneath the floor, making her legs judder. It was hard to stay upright, and all around her bodies pressed into her, swaying, sweating, arms flying, mouths open, laughing. Why were they laughing? Or were they singing? Music, that was what it was, a rhythmic sound thudding through her body; of course, she was at a party and she had to dance. She lurched forward, bouncing into the back of someone.

'Steady!' The back turned and it was Danny now, moving from side to side in front of her. She wished everybody would keep still. She'd been dancing with Danny before, moving slowly in a circle. She wanted to go back to the feel of his arms holding her close. Maybe they were on a boat? She tried to speak, but her mouth wouldn't move into the right position. Something very strange was happening to her. Air, she needed air. There was a glass of something red in her hand, and she took a long drink.

'Ava!' A flash of electric pink appeared in front of her, and recognition flickered in her mind. Her friend, she had been looking for her best friend, that was the thing she'd been trying to remember before all the noises and light started interfering. She wanted to speak, opened her mouth again, but it still wasn't working properly. She felt as if she were in a dream.

'Ava!' The brilliant pink person in front of her was speaking again, grabbing her arm, shaking it, waving a coat at her. She wanted her to stop. 'What are you doing?'

Ava's mind was full of mist again. She knew who this girl was, but she couldn't grasp her name. The word was slipping about on her tongue. Something wasn't right. The pink person pulled her arm, and a face loomed in front of her eyes. A pretty rounded face, pale skin, the mouth painted cherry red and forming words, words she couldn't catch. The face moved in and out of her vision. The pink girl was still clasping her wrist. Lena, that was it! How could she have forgotten the best friend she'd ever had?

'Lena,' she managed to say, leaning into the girl but missing and lurching forward, onto the floor. There was a tinkling sound as the glass she had forgotten was in her hand shattered, spilling bright red liquid and ice. She watched an ice cube bounce across the floor in front of her face. It would be good to sleep for a moment, she thought, but the ceiling seemed to be on a merry-go-round and she didn't know how to get off.

CHAPTER 41
Lena

'Lena, it was great to catch up.'

Relief mixes with rage as Kate throws the dart – it's a deliberate barb, but Ava follows her out seemingly without noticing as the volume of the music next door increases. When Martha speaks, however, her words are slow, her tone icy, cutting through the thumping bass of the track.

'Why does Ava think you don't know her?'

'I don't,' I say.

'Liar.' She grabs my arm, her fingernails pressing into my skin.

'Get off me.'

Her phone buzzes and I rip my arm away. She stares at the screen, an incredulous expression on her face. 'This is proof,' she says. 'I've just had a message from Ben.'

'I don't believe you. Why would he have your number?' I ask.

'I asked Mum to get him to message me. No wonder you didn't want Ava to contact him.' She holds the phone in front of my face, her fingertips colourless where she's gripping it hard. 'Don't even think about grabbing it.'

I read the screen with a sickening lurch in my stomach. I guess I'm guilty of keeping secrets too. I never told Ava about the last time Ben was over. He waited until she'd left for work. I was spreading raspberry jam on my toast and he asked if he could have a word. He stood over me, his voice soft. Said he'd never understood the power I had over Ava and that I'd been holding her back for years and it had to stop. It wasn't long after that that she told me she was off to New York, Ben smiling at her side, his arm around her waist, the glint in his eye a reminder of his words. His threat. For that was what it was.

Martha! What a surprise. Ava's party is next Saturday. Be great to catch up.

'Why does Ben think the party is next weekend, Lena?' She's shaking her head, her mouth pinched. 'This is the proof I needed. And it's not the only proof I've got, either.'

'You're mad. Proof of what? Ben's got confused, that's all.'

'Ava told me you said he didn't tell you what flight he was getting but you expected him to be here by now. Implying he was reluctant to come so she would worry. Why would you do that? You're a liar. Wait until I tell her what you've been up to. You've been seeing him, haven't you?' She reaches into her bag. 'And there's more.' She pulls out a passport. 'Look what we found in your room.'

The music gets louder, roaring in my head, and I want to stop her mouth from moving, from spilling out all her poison. My phone buzzes from where I stashed it behind the punch bowl. Martha reacts to the sound.

'Let me see your phone, Lena.' The table is vibrating, giving away its hiding place and she lunges for it. I slam my hand over hers and a bottle topples over, spilling beer all over the table. I dig my nails into her wrist, my grip claw-like. My fingers are slippery with the spilled drink.

'Stop!' Ava appears, a horrified expression on her face. 'What are you doing?'

Martha loosens her grip on my phone and I swipe it away from her.

'Your sister is deranged.' My breath comes out in fast bursts with the adrenalin of the tussle.

'She's trying to hide her phone from you, Ava. Do you know why? Tell her, Lena.'

'Shut up. You're twisting everything. Don't listen to her, Ava.'

'I've had a text from Ben. He thinks the party is next week.'

'No, he's on his way, isn't he?' Ava sounds hesitant. She frowns, looking from me to Martha as if she's watching a tennis match.

'Here's the proof.' Martha presses buttons on her phone, then holds it out to Ava, who moves towards her, strands of blonde hair falling forward over the screen.

'It's not from Ben, Ava. Don't trust her,' I say. 'She's the one who's been sending the roses.'

'She knows we've found the passport,' Martha says.

'Why was my passport hidden in your room?' Ava asks. 'Why would you do that?'

'I haven't touched your passport. Who found it?'

'Martha.'

'For someone who's supposed to be clever, Martha, you're being incredibly stupid. That's not proof of anything. She obviously planted it there, Ava. Why would I want your passport? None of this makes any sense.'

'You want to stop her going to New York. That's been obvious to me ever since I got here. Ava says you're even talking about going with her. Pathetic. Why can't you make your own way in life? You've been stuck like a leech to Ava since the first day you met her. And you've fooled everyone, even our parents, for God's sake. Ava, please, what is it going to take for me to convince you?'

'Are you seeing Ben?' Ava asks in a trembling voice.

'No, how could you think that?' My stomach twists and I feel like I'm going to be sick.

Martha is scrolling through her phone. 'Got it. There's an easy way to find out who's telling the truth. Call Ben.' She hands it to Ava. 'I bet she's taken your phone too. Go on, call him.'

Ava looks between us again, gripping the phone. 'If this is true, Lena – and I hope to God it isn't – whatever happens between me and Ben, whether I go to New York or not, I never want to hear from you again.'

She taps the screen and I'm gripped by the urge to stop her. I have to stop her. I lunge forward and grab the cake knife from the table.

'Don't touch that phone.'

Martha hurls herself towards me. 'Run, Ava!' she says. 'Get out of here. She's deranged. If anyone gets hurt here, it will be me. I won't let her touch you.'

Ava hesitates. Martha hovers, eyes fixed on mine, a glare sending a current of hatred towards me. There's a shout from the other room, and I glance to the left. My attention is only distracted for a fraction of a second, but Martha pushes Ava out of the room. She's between me and Ava, and I push the knife towards her, making contact with her arm. I have to make her stay away.

Music thuds out from the living room. A dull bump that pulses inside me along with the blood that pounds in my head. Ava's running away from me, and I have a knife in my hand. I don't know how it's come to this. Martha yells, and I shove past her, barrelling her out of the way. Ava is running, pushing through people to get to the front door. 'Go!' her sister shouts. But I won't let her go, not ever.

She has reached the front door, and is struggling to open the catch.

'Stop, Ava,' I say.

She totters, almost falling backwards as she wrenches it open and bursts forward into the street. I follow her, pausing to shut the door behind me, but I'm too late. Martha emerges clutching her arm with her hand, blood covering her fingers.

I'm aware of a roaring noise, a car engine. A white car is barrelling down the street, too fast, too loud, and I watch transfixed as Ava runs down the path, through the open gate and straight into the road.

It hits her with a sickening thump, her body flung up into the air. The squeal of tyres is deafening as the car screeches to a halt. I'm not sure whether it's Martha or me who screams loudest. For a second, everything is frozen, like a deathly version of musical statues, but the music plays on, blasting out from the house behind us.

'Oh no,' a woman says. A car door slams across the street, and it's as if a shot has been fired. Music plays out from the house as if in mockery of this horror which is unfurling. The driver appears transfixed, rigid arms gripping the steering wheel, head bowed.

'Ava,' Martha shouts and I unfreeze.

Martha gets to her first, charging over to Ava's body which lies motionless on the ground. I drop down next to Martha, her deep breathing heavy against my face as she touches Ava's forehead, where blood is colouring her hair red, spilling onto the tarmac. Horror fills me at the sight, and the years are rolling back like giant waves in my head. Martha presses her fingertips frantically to Ava's neck feeling for a pulse; my own heart is hammering in my throat, so loud I'm sure Martha can hear it too. Time slows, and it feels like I'm leaning over them forever, unable to process what I see in front of me. The car door slams.

Martha jumps to her feet. I look up, shock reverberating through me when I see who the driver is. It's like a kick to my stomach. *Kate?* She laughs and claps her hands, then swivels, preparing to run, but Martha is standing in front of her. She grabs her with bloodied hands and shoves her back against the side of the car, red streaking the white paintwork.

It's only then that I realise I'm still holding the knife, which is smeared with dark jam from the cake and I hurl it away from me, appalled. I press my shaking hands to Ava's neck, refusing to give up hope.

People are emerging from the house and I'm aware of a male voice asking for the police in a gasping tone. The music stops, and I realise the party is finally over.

'Oh my God, oh my God.' I'm repeating the phrase over and over, bending down to Ava, stroking her hair, unable to stop touching her. She's cold, but she has to be alive. She has to be. A figure kneels down beside me. It's Steph, who's brought my old raincoat from the hall. I help her cover Ava. I need to stop her getting any colder out here in the freezing temperature.

'I can't tell if there's a pulse or not,' I say, and I'm sobbing. I move my hands over her chest and start to attempt to resuscitate her, with a horrible sense of déjà vu. Steph reaches for Ava's wrist, but she doesn't say the words I need to hear.

Next to us, Martha is struggling to hold onto Kate.

Felix appears from nowhere, slamming Kate against the car. 'Call the police as well as the ambulance,' he says. Ice-cold fear slithers down my spine. Kate did this deliberately? Is that why she was here?

Martha speaks into her phone, her voice calm and authoritative, even in a crisis. She's watching Kate the whole time, and when she ends the call, she points at her.

'I know who you are,' she says, taking a step towards her. 'It's been bugging me all night. Katie Davies, Tess's little sister.' Her face crumples, and for the first time ever, I see her lose her composure, her shoulders sagging, legs faltering. 'You tried to kill my sister.'

Kate holds her stare. 'Like she killed mine,' she says coldly.

CHAPTER 42

2005

'Christ, Ava! Help me, will you, she's too heavy. Let's get her outside.'

Ava closed her eyes and allowed herself to be dragged along. Her knee banged on the floor, but she didn't feel anything. She must look really silly, hilarious even. A strange noise gurgled in her throat.

Strong hands held her arms and it was easier to walk. Then she was outside, the pulsing still there, but now it was right inside her head. What was she doing outside? She wanted to go and dance. She tried to stand, but the hands pushed her back down again. It was a boy; he was looming over her, breathing a tobacco smell into her face. A hand took hold of her chin and she was looking into a girl's face again. Lena was a girl. She giggled. Of course it was Lena, how could she have possibly forgotten? She recognised those unusual yellow-brown eyes, eyes that glinted with anger. Not at her, surely; had she done something wrong?

'Ava, listen, we need to get you home. How could you do that to me?'

'I don't want to go home,' was all she could manage.

Lena was so close to her that Ava saw a flash of annoyance contort her face, then a stinging slap against her cheek took her by surprise. Angry words were pouring out of Lena's mouth, but a loud bell was ringing in Ava's ears and the world was rotating.

She clasped her stinging cheek, staring at Lena, seeing two of her. She didn't understand what Lena was saying. Her words sounded silly, funny, and she started to laugh. She couldn't stop.

Lena grabbed her arms and pulled her to her feet. Ava swayed when she let go of her. Footsteps sounded and Ava recognised Tess as she passed them, looking in her bag for something. Lena was shouting at her, words pouring out of her mouth, but Ava still couldn't grasp them.

CHAPTER 43

Lena

'You OK?' Steph says.

'What do you think?' I say. I can't help myself.

'The ambulance is on its way.'

Steph puts her arm around me; she's shaking too. I'm rooted to the spot, unable to take my eyes off Ava's face, her ghostly pallor and the gash on her cheek where blood pools. Her angular face is lit up by the car's headlights, which cast a yellow shadow over the scene. Voices are talking quietly. I overhear people talking about her being dead and I want to tell them to shut up, but they are only saying what is in front of us. There have been too many lies tonight and it has to stop.

Minutes drag before the wail of sirens shatters the stunned silence. I become aware of people all around me; neighbours have spilled out of their houses, alerted by the awful squeal of tyres, the sickening thud that threw Ava into the air and slammed her back down on the ground. Ava, my best friend. My sister.

I'm aware that Felix is still holding on to Kate. If anyone was going to recognise her, it had to be Martha. The extra years she has on us, the time she spent with Tess, her best friend. The sirens are deafening, and then there are lights and confident voices issuing commands and I'm gently prised away from Ava, my arms aching from trying to bring her back to life. A woman is wrapping me in a foil blanket and I want to scream at her to leave me alone so I can just focus on Ava. She still hasn't moved and I can't bear to ask the question. A paramedic removes my raincoat from her and hands it to Martha, and I watch, my fist in my mouth, as he works on her. It's taking so long and I hate being so helpless. I'm aware of people moving in and out of the house, conversations muttered, a policewoman beginning to move neighbours who have come out of their houses to stare as she secures a blue and white tape with the words 'CRIME SCENE DO NOT CROSS' around the lamp posts and down the road. After what feels like forever Ava is lifted into the ambulance. Martha climbs in behind her, clutching my coat as if it will give her strength.

'Wait.' I jump to my feet to follow them, but Martha appears in the doorway of the ambulance.

'Stay away,' she says. 'You did this, the two of you; you're in this together. I saw you talking at the party. Don't let her in here.'

'No, no—' I start, but a paramedic takes my arm.

'There isn't room for both of you,' she says. 'I think it's best if you come with me. Don't worry, we'll be just behind them.'

'She's dead, isn't she?' I whisper.

The ambulance driver starts the engine, swallowing the paramedic's reply, and I only catch the end of her sentence. '… it's best if you prepare yourself for the worst.'

The paramedic tells me her name is Julia, but that's the end of the conversation and we make the rest of the journey to the hospital in silence. I follow Julia through a maze of sterile corridors as she follows instructions on her radio. We arrive at a small waiting room, where two women are talking quietly and a young man sits in the corner, his leg jigging up and down. Martha is on her phone, pacing around the room. She glares when she sees me.

'Are you two going to be all right together?' Julia asks.

'Of course,' Martha says, her stare burning into me.

I nod. 'Ava is the only thing that matters here.'

'I have to get back to the ambulance. The police will be arriving shortly to ask you a few questions. It's routine, nothing to worry about.' She squeezes my arm and she's gone.

Martha finishes her call. 'Our parents are on their way.'

'Have you seen the doctor?'

'Barely. They whisked her off as soon as we arrived. It's not looking good.' She slumps onto a chair, folds my raincoat on her lap. Dark shadows ring her eyes. 'What Kate said, it was deliberate, wasn't it? I'm going to tell the police you were in this together.'

'That's not true. You have—'

'Stop pretending. You knew Kate. You invited her to the party. I couldn't work out who she was. Then I remembered. Ava took her big sister away from her, that's how she sees it. Now she's taken my little sister. Was she behind the roses too? You have to tell me. For God's sake, Lena, Ava might die. You have to tell me what's going on.'

She fiddles with my coat, feeling around with her hands, and too late, I remember. She slides Ava's phone out of the pocket, holds it up.

'Now you have to tell me.'

I look at Martha properly for the first time. I see Ava in the angular lines of her cheekbones, the same intensity in her eyes. Then I see Ava's lifeless body. Nothing matters if she's dead. I slide to the floor and press my back to the wall, hugging my knees to my chest.

Finally I start speaking. 'Kate saw the newspaper article. She was, what, ten, eleven when the accident happened. Her big sister was her world and suddenly she was gone. She kept that article; for her it was gospel. Lena good, Ava bad. As far as she was concerned, Ava killed her big sister. You can't blame her. You hated Ava too for what she did.'

'But she's my sister. Hate and love are interchangeable in families. You wouldn't understand that.'

'You don't know me.' It's buried deep, but I can't help loving my parents, my brother, despite his choosing crime as a way of life. 'Of course I understand.' Another image takes the place of my family: a little girl, holding Tess's hand.

'I remember her,' Martha says. 'She was a shy kid, didn't have many friends.'

'And she lost the only person who'd looked out for her. She kept that article and waited. She contacted me six months later, asked to meet me. She wanted to know exactly what had happened to her sister. I was a mess at the time. Kate wanted to make sure Ava never forgot. She came up with the idea of doing something to commemorate the anniversary. The black roses were a symbol to remind Ava what she'd done. At first I tried to dissuade her; it was a crazy idea. But she kept pestering me, and the longer it went on, the more difficult it became to confess. I'd saved Ava's life and I didn't want her to ever forget. I wanted her to need me – I had no one else.

'The roses today took us both by surprise; they weren't part of the plan. Kate wasn't even meant to be at the party. But she found out Ava was leaving and she had to stop her. And when Ava assumed you were behind them, it was perfect. It could have been you. You hated her too. You've punished her for all these years.'

Martha is shaking her head, incredulous. 'What about the photographs?'

'What photographs?

'Her face has been scratched out of all the pictures in her photo album.'

'Don't be ridiculous. You might do something so hateful, but it's not my style. That must have been Kate as well. She's been messing with my head too. She threw my frame on the fire to make me think it was you doing all this. Why do you hate me so much? All I ever did was love Ava as a sister. That's all I ever wanted.'

Martha takes out a tissue and dabs at her eyes, blows her nose.

'You're right. I did hate you. I didn't trust you. I saw things our parents didn't. Ava used to tell me what you got up to when you went out. I thought you were a bad influence.'

'We were teenagers.'

'You weren't a teenager when you took the passport. Why would you do that?'

'Because I didn't want her to leave me.' My voice comes out as a wail, and one of the women in the waiting room looks across. 'None of this matters now,' I whisper. 'Nothing matters any more. You might as well know the truth.'

The sound of footsteps approaching makes me look up. A radio crackles and I hear a man's voice. Two police officers are coming towards us.

'What do you mean?' Martha asks.

I stare at the ground, focusing on a coffee stain on the grey flooring as I reveal the secret I have kept all these years. 'You were right to hate me. It was me all along, not Ava. I didn't save her life; I pushed her into the road. It was my fault Tess died.'

Martha gasps out loud and grabs my arm, her nails digging into my skin.

'Say that again.'

'It was me.'

'You.' She gasps out loud as two shiny boots move into my line of vision and I look up into the face of a police officer. Martha removes her hand, but my skin burns where her nails dug in.

'Lena Baker?'

I nod, and he speaks into his radio.

'We've got her.' To me he says, 'I'd like to ask you a few questions.'

'Oh God,' Martha says, her voice trembling. 'I've just seen your tattoo.'

I pull my dress back over the intricate image of a black rose, its petals no longer crusted with dried blood, the plaster gone. It doesn't matter any more who sees it. Ava's never going to see it now.

'Why?' Martha's voice is loud. 'Why the tattoo?' The second police officer stiffens and moves so she's standing between us. 'Let her answer me,' Martha says between gritted teeth.

'The roses bind us together, don't you see?' I say. 'Look where the tattoo is, right where her scar is, her only physical memento of that time.'

'You're mad.'

'I knew you'd never understand.'

'But she hates the black roses – wouldn't it make her suspicious, she'd think you were behind them?'

'Ava was never meant to know I was involved with sending the roses. Kate should have stuck to the rules. To me the roses were a reminder of how close we are. You know I thought she'd want me to go New York with her. I'm sure she would have changed her mind, – either taken me with her or stayed behind, she can't cope without me. And if she'd queried the tattoo I was going to tell her it was just a black and white tattoo of a rose. That it was just a coincidence and I had no idea about all the black roses over the years. And if she did leave me it was a punishment for both of us – for us not staying together, for her abandoning me; me not doing enough to keep her here. By that point, I would no longer care if she saw it and knew I was behind the roses. Because my life would be over. And now hers is too.'

'You really think she would have believed that? That it was just a coincidence?'

'I can make Ava believe anything. You know that.'

Martha shakes her head as if she thinks I'm crazy. I don't care what she thinks.

Nothing matters now that I've lost Ava.

CHAPTER 44

2005

Everything was spinning again and Lena was shouting and she wasn't sure but she thought she'd hit her and her cheek hurt and the street lights were too bright. Lena was pulling her and then she was laughing but she didn't know why.

'Come on, Ava.' Lena grabbed her arm and pulled her up, then pushed her towards the gate.

'I don't want to go home,' Ava said, shaking her arm free. The movement made her lose her balance, and she stumbled against the wall.

'We're going,' Lena said, raising her voice. Her face burned.

'No,' Ava said. 'I don't want to go.'

Lena walked through the gate and waited, her chest heaving. Ava moved towards her. Tess was getting into a car further along the street.

Lena wanted her to get into Tess's car. Lena appeared beside her, still talking but Ava's mind was fuzzy again and she folded her arms to steady herself.

'Stop telling me what to do. Danny said I don't have to do what you say. He's asked me to go to the cinema with him.'

Ava heard a car door slam.

'You know how much I like him.'

'He wants to go to university, like me. I shouldn't tell you this but he said you're not his type.'

A car brake screeched and they both turned to see the car lurch forward. Tess wasn't a very good driver.

'You can't make me leave,' she said to Lena. 'I'm going back to Danny.' The car lights dazzled Ava and made her head spin again and something pushed against her back, and she stumbled forward into the road, feeling numb as the car headed straight at her. A scraping and crashing noise roared into her head, followed by screams that weren't hers. A silent darkness descended.

CHAPTER 45

2005

Lena couldn't believe how drunk Ava was. She opened the front door and Danny helped her to get Ava outside. She sat on the floor and Danny hovered, but Lena waved at him to go back inside.

'Come on, Ava.' Lena grabbed her arm and pulled her up, then pushed her towards the gate.

'I don't want to go home,' Ava said, shaking her arm free. The movement made her lose her balance, and she stumbled against the wall.

'We're going,' Lena said, raising her voice. Her face burned.

'No,' Ava said. 'I don't want to go.'

Lena walked through the gate and waited, her chest heaving. Ava moved towards her. Tess was getting into a car further along the street.

'We can get a lift if we hurry,' Lena said.

'Stop telling me what to do. Danny said I don't have to do what you say. He's asked me to go to the cinema with him.'

A car door slammed and Lena felt her hopes shatter.

'You know how much I like him.'

'He wants to go to university, like me. I shouldn't tell you this but he said you're not his type.'

Ava's mouth was still forming words, but the sound of a car engine revving loudly, too loudly, drowned out her words. Lena couldn't bear to hear any more cruel truths from Ava; so this was how she really felt about her. Not good enough, for her or for Danny. Lena felt bruised inside, broken.

Ava moved closer.

'You can't make me leave,' she said to Lena. 'I'm going back to Danny.'

Lena was consumed by a wave of rage at her friend's stubbornness. As the headlights blazed and the car shot towards them, she ran after her, and shoved her with all her strength. The car hit Ava, swerved and veered off the road as somebody screamed. And then there was a dark and desperate silence.

CHAPTER 46

2005

Martha closed her bedroom door and leaned against it, breathing heavily. Her parents were going mad, letting that girl live with them. So what if she was a hero. Something was off with this whole situation, but God knows how she could prove it.

Tess's funeral had been the worst day of her whole life. Rain had pelted down over the funeral party, who huddled under a roof of black umbrellas. Women were draped in drab outfits in place of the colourful dresses and pastel coats they normally wore in spring. The head, Mrs Schaffer, was there along with a scattering of other teachers, but no pupils other than Tess's friends from sixth form. The school was holding a special memorial assembly, and even though much time had passed, Martha knew there would be a lot of dramatic weeping from girls who had never even known Tess. Martha kept her own grief to herself, but that didn't make her suffering any less.

The newspaper report had come out a couple of months after the funeral. A journalist from the local paper had interviewed Lena, publicising the difficult family circumstances she had grown up in. A bad-girl-come-good kind of angle, relating how Lena had pushed past her miserable childhood, which should have made her furious with the world, and performed the heroic act of rushing to save her childhood friend. When Martha had read it, the paper had ripped between her fingers she was gripping hold of it so hard, her hands shaking at the swirl of emotions roaring inside her.

'She could have told the press we wouldn't have her in the house,' her father had said, throwing a meaningful glance at her mum across the Caesar salad.

'We should invite her round here,' her mum had replied. 'Thank her at least.'

'We can do more than that.' Her dad had wiped his hands on a serviette. 'Why not ask her if she'd like to stay in the spare room until her exams are finished. Her father clearly can't cope with her, and that way he can take up the place in rehab he's been offered. She might have to go into care otherwise. That will mess up her exams completely.'

Martha had set her cutlery down on her plate, making a clattering sound.

'No, Dad. That's too much. We don't know for sure what happened.'

'Can't you read?' Ava said, pointing at the newspaper. 'She saved my life. You should be grateful to her, but no, you've always hated her.' She got up and went and threw her arms around her father. 'It's a brilliant idea, Dad, thank you. I know she'll say yes.'

That was the moment Martha knew she'd made the right decision. She was due to take up her place at Edinburgh University to study journalism next week, and she couldn't wait to get as far away from home as possible. As far away from Lena as she could.

CHAPTER 47

Ava

We meet in Central Park. I'm here early, well wrapped up in a faux-fur coat and hat, a woollen scarf covering most of my face; I needed time to sit and prepare myself. Ben offered to come with me, to take the day off work – he'd do that for me, but not in the self-sacrificing way Lena used to. I shudder when I think of her. I try not to, but she's still always there, lurking at the edge of my thoughts.

When I came round in the hospital, they told me I'd been unconscious for a week and that my family had been advised to prepare themselves for the worst. When they mentioned my sister, I thought at first they meant Lena, and then it all flooded back. Lena was not my real sister. Martha was at the party ... A sharp pain seared through my head. *The party.* Short sequences of memories returned to me, each one causing the pain to worsen. I cried out, and the nurse rushed over. She told me I was on morphine and that she could adjust the dose if I was hurting, and I just about managed to nod my throbbing head. The drug erased the memories and I preferred the semi-conscious state of drowsing to the clarity I experienced on waking.

Ben was the first person I saw, his hands holding onto mine, warm, solid. He had to be part of a dream, and I closed my eyes quickly, wanting to stay with him. But his gentle voice was persistent, repeating my name, telling me how he'd rushed to be with me as soon as he got the news; how he'd thought the party was next week, how Lena had misled him. Lena. Hearing her name made me open my eyes, my chest full of restless moths, and struggle to sit up, but Ben calmed me down, called the nurse, who reassured me I was safe.

'You were right,' I told him, 'about Lena.'

He nodded. 'You know I always trust my gut, and there was something disturbing about her. She hated me being around you; she tried to hide it, but I could tell. That's why I got you to change your plans that time you were both supposed to be coming to visit. But she can't hurt you now. And I'm not leaving the UK until you're on that plane coming back with me.'

After that, Mum was there every time I opened my eyes; I later learned I'd woken for the first time on one of the rare occasions she'd been persuaded to take a break from her vigil and had gone home to sleep. She gave herself a hard time for missing me coming round and refused to leave after that until I was out of danger. *Danger.* I had felt as if I was in danger most of my life. Was it over at last?

The doctor arrived with his clipboard and went over my injuries with me: broken collarbone and ribs, deep bruising all over. But none of that mattered, because the scar had stopped hurting. My fingers brushed over it every now and then to be sure, but there was nothing. The raised skin was still smooth against my fingers, but it didn't throb any longer. Lena had gone from my life and taken the pain with her.

I've selected my favourite spot in the park: a bench with a view over the lake. The trees are covered with a white dusting of snow and the bitter cold is a constant surprise. The lake is partially frozen. Tall buildings fill the skyline surrounding the park and I feel protected knowing they are there. No way could this park be in London – I like to remind myself where I am.

Martha has been in constant contact. She was there with Mum the day I woke, and I realised the time had come to start living again. But first I had to ask the question that had been there since I'd opened my eyes.

'Where is she?'

I didn't need to say her name; her presence hung over every one of us in the hospital room. The last thing I could remember was Lena threatening me with a knife and Martha telling me to run, followed by a screeching sound and a white flash turning to black in my head.

'She isn't allowed in,' Mum said. 'You don't need to worry about her while you're in here. The police will want to speak to you about the accident and it will be up to you whether you press charges or not.'

'Press charges?'

They helped me piece together what had happened. Kate was the mastermind of all this; Kate Davies, little Kate, Tess's younger sister, who I could barely remember. Mum brought a photo in at my request to remind me. Kate had known I wouldn't recognise her; why would I? Our paths had never intersected. My big sister's best friend's little sister – she was nobody to me, an insignificant child. A girl of around ten or eleven in school uniform with a solemn stare and a badly cut fringe looked out of the photograph at me, a complete stranger.

It turned out that that little girl had kept the newspaper cutting about the accident, enlisting Lena to help her punish the person who had caused her sister's death. Me. Only it wasn't me. That's the hardest part to take in in all of this: that guilt I've carried around my whole life was completely unnecessary; it didn't belong to me. It belonged to Lena.

'It makes sense to me now, in a warped kind of way,' Martha said. 'I can see how Lena rationalised it: by keeping the accident alive in your mind and feeding your guilt and shame, you'd continue to need her in your life. Kate getting in touch with her, wanting revenge, had reminded her of all that she stood to lose once she'd wormed her way into our family.' Mum looked distressed at this and I squeezed her hand; Lena had fooled us all. All of us except for Martha. A wave of love for my sister washed over me. My real sister.

'You going off to Cambridge terrified her,' Martha said, 'but she managed to cling onto you, to stay in your life. Until New York and Ben took the threat to a whole other level.'

'But why did she invite Kate to the party?' I asked.

'She didn't. Kate followed the crowd from the office in and she told Steph she was with some guy she was seeing in Accounts. Why wouldn't Steph believe her – quite a few people brought partners she hadn't met before. It was actually Pete who invited her.'

'Pete?'

'Kate made it her business to get to know him. She seduced him and persuaded him to give you a hard time at work. It was all part of her campaign of revenge.'

'That's so twisted,' I said, shock reverberating through me.

'Her sister's death had been eating her up for years. She planned all this carefully. It suited her that Lena was so attached to you. The party was Lena's last way of holding onto you. She'd tricked Ben into thinking it was the following weekend and hidden your phone; she wanted you to believe he couldn't be bothered to come. She had no idea Kate would turn up; she swears she didn't know she meant to harm you. Then me showing up fed into her rage, and finding out that you were engaged and planned to go abroad for good sent her over the edge. I think that's why she grabbed the knife. That wasn't planned; I saw it happen.'

Martha shrugged. 'We wind each other up, always have done, probably always will. The woman's a mess; she needs professional help. Kate trying to kill you was never in her plan, though, I believe that.' She let out a groan. 'It was awful. She thought you were dead, Ava, we all did.' She sat down on the edge of the bed suddenly, as if she'd run out of breath. 'I'm so glad you're still alive.' She laughed nervously.

'Did you realise who Kate was?' I asked.

'It dawned on me just after she'd left. It had been bugging me – obviously she looked very different to when I'd last seen her, but she was often there when I was round at Tess's house. She was always badgering Tess to let her join in with us. It's sad really, she idolised her sister and it used to drive Tess mad. Not that it excuses what she did; nothing ever could. But Tess dying hit her hard – hit us all hard. And it had nothing to do with you.'

A flash of red against the white background jolts me out of my reverie. Martha strides towards me, elegant in a long red coat, beret placed at a jaunty angle on her head. Chic even in the snow, making me feel like an explorer in comparison. I get up to embrace her, and she hugs me tightly before stepping back and appraising my face.

'You look so much better, despite the arctic conditions.' We sit down on the bench. 'Jeez, it's cold. Hot chocolate will be needed after this. How are you getting on here in the Big Apple? Glad you made the move?'

I look around me at the park that has become so familiar over the past few weeks.

'Oh yes, I feel settled.' Unlike the snow, which covers the grass in a dazzling white blanket for a finite time, I plan on staying here, putting down roots. I love the whirl of the city, where I am anonymous. 'I'm grateful to be making a fresh start.'

'Have you heard about Kate? Or would you rather not know the verdict?'

'Yes, my police contact from the case got in touch.'

'Dangerous driving was all she got, a two-year sentence, can you believe; she'll be out in a few months. The jury found her not guilty of grievous bodily harm – there wasn't enough evidence to convince them. We did our best; I'm only sorry we couldn't get a better result for you. Though I've heard through her barrister that she is repentant and has agreed to undergo psychiatric treatment, something that should have happened years ago.'

Kate's getting the help she needs, but what about Lena? I won't contact her again, but I can't help wondering.

'Are you worrying about Lena?' It's as if Martha can read my mind. 'There's no need to, she didn't get bail. She can't get to you any more.'

'Why is it taking so long to go to trial?'

Martha shrugs. 'That's the British justice system for you. At least she's pleading guilty to Tess's manslaughter.'

'Yes, that makes me feel better. I'm completely exonerated. Have you heard from her?' I ask.

Martha looks aghast. 'No, why would I? I never want to see her again and I hope you don't either.' She raises an eyebrow in question.

I shrug. Martha stamps her feet.

'It's freezing. Shall we walk a bit? You can show me around this fabulous park. Do you know, I've been to New York on so many business trips and never had time to come here.' She links her arm with mine. 'I want to hear all about your wedding preparations.'

As we walk, I mull over the conversation I had with Ben last night. He was all for my suggestion and I smile at the thought. Small steps are taking me along the path in the right direction. Keep on going, and I'll get there. I know that now. I believe in myself and the choices I'm making. And this is definitely my choice.

'Funny you should mention the wedding,' I say. 'Ben and I were just discussing it last night. We'd like you to be my chief bridesmaid.'

Martha stops and looks at me. 'Oh Ava, I'd love to. Are you sure?'

'Of course.' I laugh and we hug each other again. 'We need to make up for lost time. You can come for longer then, stay in our apartment while we're on honeymoon if you like.'

'You're on – as long as it's a bit warmer when you get married.' She links her arm in mine again. 'Come on, this definitely calls for a hot chocolate – followed by cocktails.'

CHAPTER 48
Lena

They all think they understand, that they've got me sussed, understand my psychological motivation, whatever fancy words they want to dress it up in. I would never have tried to hurt Ava a second time. I just wanted to stop her leaving. But thanks to Kate, I failed, and now we're both locked up, paying for it. Life has never been fair and I was stupid to think I deserved a second chance.

Like she killed mine. Little Kate Davies, all grown up, solemn eyes replaced by a hard expression, a determination to do right by the sister she loved. We're very alike. Both of us wanting to punish Ava.

I shoved her so hard that night, a lifetime of rage and envy coursing through my veins and bursting out in a bolt of energy into my hands, propelling Ava into the road and in front of the car. They say you hurt those you love; well, in that moment I wanted to hurt Ava. But hurting so many others besides her, that wasn't expected. The person I hurt most was myself, and living with the knowledge of what I did and keeping Ava from ever finding out has shaped my life.

Tess didn't stand a chance. Her driving test fresh in her mind, she attempted to stop the swerve with an emergency stop, practised so carefully, but in real time the car veered out of control, no match for a slight teenager. All this I found out later, from the police, or was it the hospital staff – everything that happened afterwards is a blur – who were nothing but kind to me because all they saw was me saving Ava's life. And I did save her life. Nobody can take that away from me. The minute I saw her like a broken doll on the ground, my hate snapped back into love and I did everything I could to revive her.

As for recent events, in the whirl of emotions in the immediate aftermath, Martha and I were both raw and the truth was exposed. She saw my tattoo and it all came tumbling out. Everything she'd ever thought about me was true. But in that moment of rare togetherness, when we both feared the worst, it felt right to bare myself to her, because she loved Ava too and we could see that about each other.

Speaking to Martha was unexpectedly cathartic, although I'm not sure she understood about the tattoo. Warped maybe, but it made perfect sense to me. Knowing it was happening, that Ava was leaving me, despite the roses, despite the plan I'd conjured up with Kate, I had the tattoo imprinted into my shoulder at the exact spot where she had her scar; the only visible legacy of the accident. That scar gave her so much pain, and I welcomed the torturous drilling of the tattooist. It was a permanent reminder to me of what I'd done.

Being locked up gives me too much time to think. I still don't know whether Ben has told her; maybe I'll never know. It happened last Christmas, when Ava was doing some last-minute shopping. He came downstairs in his dressing gown, and I couldn't help myself. Never could resist a good-looking man, me. It was only the once, and I could tell immediately that he regretted it; he wouldn't look me in the eye. It didn't mean anything to me and it certainly didn't to him; he made that clear when he threatened me on his last trip over, warning me to stay away from Ava. Big mistake. I wouldn't have stopped him from coming to the party if he hadn't done that.

I love Ava, you see, and he isn't good enough for her. Everything I did I did for love. By the time I get out, she'll be back. She'll have found out what he's really like and I'll be here for her. I'll still be waiting.

A LETTER FROM LESLEY

Thank you so much for reading *The Leaving Party*. I hope you enjoyed reading it as much as I enjoyed writing it. If you did enjoy it, and want to keep up to date with all my latest releases, just sign up at the following link. Your email address will never be shared and you can unsubscribe at any time.

www.bookouture.com/lesley-sanderson

As with my first two books, *The Orchid Girls* and *The Woman at 46 Heath Street*, I hoped to create an evocative novel about obsession, secrets and the blurred lines between love and lies. In this book, having the action unfold within one evening added an extra level of intrigue. Once again, female relationships lie at the heart of my novel, enhanced by the suppression of secrets.

If you enjoyed *The Leaving Party*, I would love it if you could write a short review. Getting reviews from readers who have enjoyed my writing is my favourite way to persuade other readers to pick up one of my books for the first time.

I'd also love to hear from you via social media: see the links below.

www.lesleysanderson.com

@LSandersonbooks

lsandersonbooks

ACKNOWLEDGEMENTS

So many people have helped me along the way with *The Leaving Party*.

I'd like to share my appreciation of my fellow Curtis Brown Creative classmate Neil McLennan, who sadly passed away this year. Neil gave me huge support with his feedback and witty observations and I will forever miss his encouragement and lovely personality.

Thanks to the wonderful people of the Lucy Cavendish Fiction Prize for short-listing me for the 2017 prize, for the kindness of everyone involved with the event and their continued support.

To my lovely agent and Bookseller Rising Star of 2019, Hayley Steed, and to everyone else at the fabulous Madeleine Milburn agency. Hayley, your continued belief in me means the world, and I love your energy and enthusiasm.

To the Next Chapter Girls – Louise Beere, Clêr Lewis and Katie Godman – you know how much you and this writing group mean to me; I couldn't have done it without your belief in me and my writing.

To my lovely editor Christina Demosthenous – working with you is a joy. To everyone at Bookouture – especially Kim, who does my fabulous publicity – and Alex – you all work tirelessly and with infectious enthusiasm for your authors, and I'm so proud to be one of them.

And to everyone else – all the other writers I've met along the way, too many to name but nonetheless important – I'm so happy to be one of such a friendly group of people.

To my family, to my friends old and new for believing in me, I daren't name you in case I miss anyone out, but thank you.

And most of all, to Paul. I couldn't do it without you.

Printed in Great Britain
by Amazon